Orca

A LITERARY JOURNAL

Issue 5, Autumn 2020

orcalit.com

Orca, A Literary Journal
Number 5
Autumn 2020

ISBN-13: 978-1-942797-25-8

A cursory glance at this issue's stories seems to yield a disturbing thread. In fact when we were curating the story order one of the staff quipped we should subtitle this "The Violence Issue." We begin with shotguns, and move into hunting, disease, prize fighting, cockfighting, Russian roulette, rape, police abuse, headless dolls, and an alligator with knife stuck in its head.

Phew.

Fortunately, readers of literary journals aren't much into cursory glances. These stories may have their bases in violent acts, but each is in fact a probing exploration of the humanity that persists in the wake of the world's violence—apart from it, despite it, and far more powerful in the long run.

Read. Think. Enjoy.

– Joe, Zac, Renee, Marci, David, Zoë, Ronak, Tommy

Editor's Note: We have not Americanized spellings and grammar native to other English-speaking countries, but have left them in their original form in order to fully convey the voices of our authors.

Orca

A LITERARY JOURNAL

Contents

About the Cover

From Miranda's Show at Causey Contemporary in NY.

"(W)e are often encouraged to pay too much attention to someone else's work."

This simple statement helps explain why our cover artist, Francisco Miranda of Buenos Aires, is able to work across so many artistic genres.

And spectacularly so.

New Zealand stamp designs.

In addition to painting and illustration, Miranda is well accomplished in creative 3-D design and commercial art, having produced works for entities ranging from the Sharjah Art Museum in the United Arab Emirates, to Microsoft and Campari, to the New Zealand Post Office, galleries throughout the world, and even for the reality show "Big Brother Argentina."

As the son of an electro-mechanical engineer and a bohemian writer, he tends to approach his projects from a mathematical viewpoint. "There's just something about the Spreadsheet, the process, the math behind it all," he says.

His career began as a graphic designer. Miranda studied at the University of Buenos Aires, where he taught for seven years after receiving his degree. He also worked in design and illustration for several studios and advertising agencies, but soon began questioning his art. That led him to experiment with different materials and techniques, realizing, at some point, that he needed to evolve from two-dimensional art into disruptive "volumetric" works. Specialization in a single area of art is, he says, is limiting.

Artwork for Campari, and the print ad.

He takes his inspiration from "animals big and small, real and imaginary. In plants and insects. Heaven. Books. Ink. Inanimate objects. Machines and their gears. Taking apart and reassembling. Looking back and to the sides. Molecules, numbers, the abstract. Constant travelling. Being here and there at the same time. Planets. Experiments. The chemistry and physics. Infinity."

Additional samples of Francisco Miranda's work and contact information are at www.tooco.com.ar, www.franciscomiranda.com.ar, and www.facebook.com/tooco.

Francisco Miranda in his studio.

About th Cover

3

4

Sisters of the Shotgun

STEPHANIE DICKINSON

In the beginning of my second life my hair was short. I had to grow my brunette hair shoulder-length; the scar wouldn't show as much. I needed to be able to hide my cheek, the place where the pellets went in, buckshot from a 12-gauge shotgun blast that made a hole, took jawbone and teeth, formed a zipper of scar. I imagined a white crane spreading his flight feathers and those would be the white sutures, the marks and dents in my face. I pictured black cranes roosting on my paralyzed left arm, on the pieces of shot and each of my fisted fingers.

I am used to feeling singular having met only one other one-armed girl. She too had two arms, but one was paralyzed. So I will think about Mary and try to remember her. I'll conjure up the year after graduate school when I'd signed up to become a Volunteer in Service to America, a VISTA, and moved to Colorado Springs where my assignment was to organize a Disabled Rights Coalition. The scar is part of my soft underbelly, the dent in my cheek, and the more scar under my hair. The scar runs like rickrack from the corner of my mouth over my jaw where the bone is gone and then divides into two trickling streams on my neck. Shrapnel still inside my left eyelid make its own purplish shadow. The wounds themselves don't forget the blast, they do not age.

I sit in the passenger's seat watching Michael, our project director, comb his wispy beard with the fingers on his right hand while steering with the fingers on his left hand. We're on the road to Salida, a mountain town on the front range. I am not really watching him anywhere but in my mind's eye and I can't tell you all the rich details I've forgotten. Michael has the look of a winner, newly married but still sporting his campus look, a jacket over a t-shirt, jeans, and the reddish beard. We head west through Manitou Springs passing dry lakes rimmed by boulders in tenuous balance. Sometimes the landscape makes a deeper impression than people, scenery can gouge a hole in you and fill it with pleasure or pain. Each boulder pitched at angles. The foothills. Mushroom-like rocks rise on elongated stems into caps while others rest on stocky trunks and finish in a flourish of tabletop, magpies nesting in them. I am bringing Michael back as I am bringing myself at twenty-three forward. I will start here and work my way to eighteen, the first year of my mutilation, the hardest. The year I was eighteen seemed to last forever, I could not turn nineteen until I spoke again with the angel of death. That is why I am telling you about twenty-three, I am telling you about twenty-three because it's so much easier.

Eighteen was the darkness spread over the river. The year of lying curled in the dirt and rocking myself. The year my breasts ached, they felt like a milk can had filled them, they could bleed through the front of my shirt. It was the year the literal and metaphorical fused, no minnows or earthworms, only spit on a bare hook. What might I catch with pieces of my own flesh? Cut bait. Dangerous currents. Eighteen was the year of rocky crevices sheltering blasphemers and rapists. A year of blue ice and hot nights and the monsters sleeping like babies in wife beaters and stocking caps. The year of a mouth wired shut and bone-deep grief. The struggle to keep my spirit inside a shattered self. So you see how much easier is age twenty-three.

Sisters of the Shotgun

Age eighteen she was coming back to life after a hard winter. Maimed for three months—first hospital, then rocking herself in her aunt's closet, imagining she'd somehow bring back the girl who was. She was halved—wet feathers lopped in goo and brine, a second birth, waiting for teeth to break from her gums, for ears to understand sounds that had not yet become words, or thoughts scoured from the bramble. She awoke here, sensed a toughness to this land that ran feral like the numbness in her cheek and chin, the metal in her jaw, the shrapnel scattered in her lungs, the tubes forced down her windpipe.

"You're going to really like Mary," Michael says "You have a lot in common. You'll really get to know her in Denver at the conference." I know she's another raw recruit tasked with scraping up the disabled and making them into a coalition. We're picking her up and then driving to Denver for the symposium. I know Michael has used the suspect word *really,* twice in three short sentences. I recall that obscure detail because I scribbled it down. "She has the use of one arm like you." He assumes the one-armed will embrace like sisters. Compadres. I want to ask how she became one-armed, stroke, accident, birth but am shy and busy lighting another cigarette between swallows of Coke.

A cigarette goes well with gazing out the window at the passing junipers, their limbs and branches spare like the soil isn't strong enough to feed them. Something about my supervisor feels weak as well. So ardent, smart, and a believer in human rights causes, yet too shiny and successful, as if he hasn't been kicked in the face or bruised enough. The snowcapped Rockies rise on the horizon, each peak, a strange god. The country becomes more scrub pine and wind-scoured. We reach the edge of Salida and the Loyal Duke Lodge beckons travelers.

The trailer sits by itself in the trees and we park and walk on ground softened by thousands of pine needles. Mary holds the aluminum screen for us and greets us with a wide smile and howdy in the front range style. I can hear the banging of the flimsy screen after we pass inside, the wind catching it and then blowing it shut. She dresses in jeans and a t-shirt but I've forgotten the color, the fit, although on her wrist, the right one, she wears a man's silver watch, the time face oversized, like a miniaturized kitchen clock. When Mary comes to mind in all the years since the forearm and watch appear first. "My two kids are in school and my fiancé is working on our new house." Even with her kids in school the trailer feels crowded. Stuffed with trophies and statuettes, bursting at the seams but clean, the plywood walls a stampede of velour horses and canyons. Large-breasted and short, rich chocolate hair, she stands in the tiny kitchen squeezing dish soap on a pyramid of plates and pans. I watch her mouth as she speaks in her friendly twang. I do not want to give her *the look* but I want to know. Yes, she deftly handles the plates and silverware with one hand, her left one. Her right arm the one wearing the watch is the one that doesn't work, and Mary lifts it and places her forearm on the edge of the sink. The thing we share. Who will be the first to ask the other what happened? She laughs, stacks a dish in the drainer, and picks up her cigarette smoldering in a nearby horse-shoe ashtray. A girl after my own heart.

"Are you Italian?" I ask.

"Part Italian," she says, "Part Scottish, French, Italian, and Lakota Sioux. My daddy is the Lakota French piece. Hey, how old are you?"

"Twenty-three. You?"

"Twenty-five. I'm going to stay twenty-five, I've decided."

We ask the easy questions not the real ones.

Twenty-three is not the age of walking with my head down or holding hair over my scar as the wind tries to expose the left side of my face. Twenty-three is an unwired mouth, hair to the middle of my back, longer, twenty-three is two scar revisions later, the zipper broken into zigzags to fade into the shape a face naturally takes. Twenty-three, a girl glued back together can enjoy the wind and how lightning shakes from the sky. Hoops in my ears, a black satin jacket, stovepipe black pants, sling back heels.

Maybe Michael is using the tinker toy bathroom, because he's not there, and then he is. "I want to show you our new house and introduce you to Bo, my fiancé," Mary informs him, grinning. Straight white even teeth. No facial scars.

She is beautiful.

I wonder now if her eyes linger anywhere on me. Usually, I hold my arms crossed over my chest but today I carry a notebook in the crook of my left arm. I try to disguise my gimpness, I try to pretend I'm able-bodied. Render an arm useless then set it on fire. Mary seems natural in her own hide. I am locked in a skin of self-consciousness. We pile into Mary's truck. She drives the old stick-shift Mountaineer, reaching over with her left hand to work the shifter. She shifts by resting her right hand on the steering wheel and shifting with her left. She is a lightning woman.

I'm drawn even now to the oddness of the house, asymmetrical, aslant. The kitchen painted green, the cabinets crookedly indigo, and the cupboards lined with blue cornflower cupboard paper. Nothing matches. My kind of place. Her fiancé, shirtless and white with crumbling plaster, shows us how he's busted the walls open and the old lathes poke through. "I'm getting down to the bones," Bo says, proudly, his grin as crooked as the cabinets. "Say goodbye to your wall, baby. I'm about to break it down." Blond and scruffily hand-some, the All-American rodeo bronco rider, he gives off the warm smell of tar and pine. Mary faces the smattering of holes and pellets embedded in the remaining wall. "I hate to let them go." She points to the rivulets of white that run through the grimy blue paint. "We scrubbed the gooey stuff off." Michael stays in the house chatting with Bo, while Mary and I head outside.

The junipers have been devastated by fire. Mary and I shuffle over scorched patches of earth into the black trees. "The birds didn't come back yet," she says. "Some of them tried to fly with their wings on fire. Feathers burn like hair. They light up, then poof, they're gone."

It seems fitting that we talk about our own burning here. "So how did it happen with you?" I ask.

Stephanie Dickinson

"We were drinking and partying in the house. My brothers and their girlfriends were over and the more we drank, the more it seemed like fun to do some shooting. I picked up my youngest brother's shotgun and aimed at the wall and shot a piece of myself while I was at it," she says, flatly. A minute later she's laughing.

But how unmarked she is, unlike me.

Will she tell me how her body felt being hurled into space? I rarely share that sensation, never to outsiders, only to friends who witness the burning neurological pain that keeps me awake nights. Pulses of erratic electricity that handfuls of Advil only blunt. Was it surprise at the close range shotgun blast before blacking out? Nothing sexy about the gun unlike the craze and soft I feel for my eighteen-year-old self's shoulders and neck and hair or the pillows of her lips.

In Denver we share a hotel room at the Radisson. We sit in a back row table at the symposium and drink free coffee and open our heavy three ring binders filled with the full-length Section 504 Regulations of the Rehabilitation Act of 1973. We use yellow markers, while painstakingly the lawyers, paraplegics mostly and polished public speakers, review the Regs, one after another after another. The wheelchair lawyers weave anecdotes from their lives through the government-speak and we are riveted. We eat our salad lunches together and nights in the hotel bar we guzzle Tom Collins because Mary also likes the fruity weirdness of the drink. We learn how wide the stalls in handicapped bathrooms need to be, which agencies are required to pony up the cash to put in ramps. Once the symposium ends and I lug the three-ring binder home, I never open it again.

I like Mary. We are sisters of the shotgun. After the afternoon session ends and we drink our sissified Tom Collins topped with a cherry, Mary announces she wants to go to a porn movie. She finds an address in the yellow pages and off we go. I remove my glasses before entering the grim little theater with no popcorn or licorice for sale in the deep red lobby. I want not to see. We brush through the curtain that serves as a door and behind it the rows and a sprinkling of men are slouching in their seats, their heads and shoulders barely showing. The theater is perfumed with piss and Lysol. I notice no couples sit together and we seem to be the only women. In fact, no men take seats next to each other. Murkiness. Each asks for his own privacy, his own elbow room in the gloom. Some loners own a whole row. Like fishermen in their flatboats, oars lifted from the thick green water. Nothing biting. Yet mesmerized. We walk down the aisle into stillness, a weekday mass. Mary leads the way and since she wants to miss nothing plops down in the front row. The mile-high city soon disappears, the thin atmosphere, and smell of blue spruce.

On the screen flickering with motes there's a repairman who calls himself Spartacus. His arms hardened by exercise seem obscene in their bulges. His member erect. The girl must be of age because of her balloon breasts but the rest of her seems a skinny thirteen-year-old with a ponytail of long black hair and pale eyebrows. Spartacus is potbellied and goat hair mats his thick shoulder blades. The film jitters, the camera must be hand held. The hero stands by a bed, his palm pushing the ponytail girl to her knees before him. The girl gags at the crinkly hair his penis nests in. It looks like a smelly curl of worms.

We walk out and blink at the light, almost surprised that the sun is still up. Seated in the dingy theater I forgot that day might still be going on outside. I kept picturing myself at age eighteen, seven months after the shooting, down on my knees at a rest stop before a stranger who paid me $20 for a blowjob.

"What did you think of the film, Mary?" I ask as we start down the sidewalk heading west into the Denver dusk.

She laughs, crinkling the corners of her brown eyes. "I thought it was a hoot. I can't wait to tell Bo all about it. We like to experiment."

From there we head to a trophy shop whose address she found. "I want to get an engraving done on a trophy for my son. He won his first wrestling match after a long time trying. I guess we eat too many peanut butter sandwiches and cupcakes at home and my baby got a little chunky."

And so we stroll the six blocks as the sun sets, the altitude and pollution turning the sun into a crimson fireball surrounded by purples and pinks, a tableau of bruises. Looking into the shop windows we pass, I glimpse two shotgun girls in a glaze of blue maroon. The last of the light on my skin feels like warm water. I can't stop seeing Spartacus, the cruel sexual gladiator, pressing the head of ponytail girl, keeping her on her knees before him. His member, his pitiless scepter. I keep hearing the gagging, choking noises the girl made. The camera watching her work the tiny lines around her mouth.

Age eighteen is the year of blizzards, the sky heavy and snow like pellets of shot, snow riding the wind like frantic fucking, no monarch butterflies gathering in the wing-shaped dark clouds. It is the year of humidity, fingers clenching and on fire, the head bowing to the electric shock. Age eighteen weighs ninety pounds. Age eighteen is barefoot, unbuttoning, and wanting to please. It's the year of hitchhiking in ripped jeans, orchid lipstick, black eyeliner and scars. The year of dragonflies, the beautiful killers, their wings of steel slivers. The year I pick at the fingers of my left hand until they bleed. I will be twenty-three when a doctor finally tells me I am trying to scratch life back into them.

When I think about age twenty-three I see how the lights die behind us as the highway reaches higher into the mountains. Soon we will drop Mary off at her trailer among the junipers and pines. She's explained to us how the blue juniper berry is really a tiny cone, not a fruit. She'll want no help gathering up her overnight case, her three-ring seminar binder, the engraved trophy for her wrestling son, and her shopping bags. It's after midnight and the trailer is dark. Mary manages to open the door, turn with her packages, and wave. Swallowing hard, I wave back. I ride with Michael for hours through the Colorado night. "Hey, look," he says, "there's a shooting star." I follow his finger pointing to the arc of a meteor burning as it falls to earth. I never see Mary again.

Stephanie Dickinson

A Fall Play: In One Act and Three Scenes

DAVID LUNTZ

Scene I. Cabin. Farm and woods. Late October.

Beyond my porch, a violent gust scatters leaves toward the afternoon light. The last train of butterflies flees south. A lone hawk rides a thermal, spiraling upwards. The sky spreads over us, as if just yanked from infinity, still bleeding from its blue umbilicus. Straggling bands of cirrus cinch the wound.

The shot came from four hundred yards away, past the stream, up in the trees. I hear the dull thud of a bullet punching through flesh. The hawk dips slowly into the wind. From that height, it would see who took the shot: bolt action, hollow point, 33 grain, fifteen pounds of recoil energy. I've been around enough guns most of my eighty years to know.

The shooter was going for the heart but misjudged the spin drift. I stumble down the porch steps, cursing. I can't be doing this. My hip is busted. I wonder, *Why'd he do it from so far away?* Fucking amateur. I stagger through a grove of spruces. Spider webs sway from their gibbets. Some stick to my face. Husks of blowflies sprinkle the ground, like pistachio shells tossed from idle spectators at a hanging. There's a maple tree up right ahead, a blazing loom, spinning gold leaves. Each step I take to it is discovering some new land in an uncharted world of agony. At last, I gasp against the tree, shaking. My daughter is buried below it. I mouth a broken prayer to her. I'm not sure why. I talk to her all the time.

A bear claw has left a two-inch gash in the trunk. I smooth the bark around it, trying to mend the deformity. I lick my fingers. They taste like quinine, medicinal. It doesn't help my pain. Beneath the bear gash, though, swims a sweet sap, as sweet as the inside of a hummingbird's throat. Like hope buried beneath a thick rind of despair. I dig my nails into it, trying to scratch my way to that sugar. I've been trying to do that my whole life. But there's no time now. Forty yards away, more like forty miles, I wobble over to the wood-shed. My body is going numb. On the floor, a cratered bee hive conceals the rusted spoke of a wheelbarrow. A shovel and a twelve-inch serrated blade sit in its cracked tub. I reach down for them. Time to bury mistakes.

Scene II. Fields. Hilltop clearing. Late October

Outside again, another wave builds up far away. I feel it in my knees. The ebbing away of air, the sudden drop of pressure, exposes a jagged shore of beetled carapaces choking up ruts in my fields. I am crawling over them. I have no strength to stand and walk. In my chest, hoof-beats gallop over crooked ribs, down a warped plank of spine. The pain is so bad I roll on my back for a moment to scream. I am drenched in sweat. The hawk is still up there, absorbing everything. Space suspends into stillness, as it does during an eclipse. I sense the air, like an invisible sleeve, getting turned inside out, summer's dead skin slipping away. I am passing through one season into another, getting turned inside out too, belly sliding now up a hill, dragging the spade behind me with one hand, clawing the earth in front with the other, the sharp metallic taste of steel clenched in my teeth.

15

David Levintz

The summit has a clearing where they always come to die. With a final push, I sliver through the undergrowth to the open ground. There it lies. Just as I thought: the hole four centimeters away from the heart. Not clean. Large black eyes plead with me. They are confounded by existence. I sense we are approaching each other from different universes, but will converge on the same thought. I sit up and cradle its head in my lap. I stroke its neck. Its eyes are like my daughter's beneath the blazing tree.

I sing it a lullaby, the same I sang to her every night. Its wheezing slows down, as if it's going to sleep. Maybe the song earns my trust. Maybe it understands my pain too. Maybe it's too tired to care. For a moment the three of us are together. My mouth tastes like salt. My eyes burn. The creature goes still. The knife won't be needed.

The wave breaks and showers us in leaves. The ground here is brittle and crusted like old scabs. The shovel will help me to stand up. I know it will break when I dig the grave.

Scene III. Woods. Hilltop Clearing. Late October

There is a crack, like close thunder. There is pain with no previous memory. There is panic. There is a place I must get to. There is a dark cloud of flies who smell my blood. There is sunlight going cold on my back. There is a hawk watching from above. There is a hill and the baked scent of earth. There is a clearing where I can now go to sleep. A shadow crawls over me, panting and groaning. It smells sickly. It grips my head and howls as my children do when they are lost. It weeps into my mouth. The tears carry something sweet, something I have sought my whole life but never tasted. The water that flows deep inside the tree whose leaves turn to fire when the days grow short.

My Mother on Film

NATASHA MARKOV-RISS

In eighth grade, I got caught skipping school three days in a row. My homeroom teacher called up my mother and told her that *the three of us must have a little chat.* It was Saturday morning, but Ms. Pieri said she would unlock the middle school just for us. I found that terribly ominous.

My mother barely looked at me during breakfast. She sat in the car listening to NPR while I tied my shoes. I glanced over at her while we were driving to school, craving a thaw, but her jaw was as hard as I'd ever seen it. She talked to my Uncle Colin and Aunt Sylvia on the phone, didn't put them on speaker or gesture for me to say *hi.*

After Ms. Pieri invited us to sit down, she produced spiteful phrases like *Lydia has skipped three days of school this week* and *we are concerned she is not a good fit for this community.* It made the spot in between my lungs tingle with hatred. I stared at the cold, unused fireplace behind her chair.

Then my mother looked at me. She gave me a little smile and turned back to Ms. Pieri.

What's the problem with skipping school? That's what she asked Ms. Pieri. *What's the problem with skipping school?*

Ms. Pieri looked at my mother like she had asked for a sexual favor.

I'm sorry, what? My mother's words had snapped a tendon inside Ms. Pieri's taut little heart. I could see the two halves of it jumping away from each other, the way a guitar string would if you cut it with scissors. My mother was smiling.

What's the problem with Lydia skipping school? School's not the only place to learn. (My days off were spent smoking behind the abandoned office complex, which my mother certainly knew.)

Ms. Pieri recovered a little, tied her tendon back together the way you tie a broken rubber band, and said, *Linda, these are our rules. She would need a note from a parent or guardian.*

So my mother reached over, took a sticky note off of Pieri's pad, and said, *Consider this my note.* It was like a movie. *Consider this my note.*

Her messy scrawl. That, I never forgot.

Professor Nobal wrote mostly in cursive, smooth and slanted. She would stand at the head of the long oak table and read her hand-written lecture notes from the yellow legal pad, pausing to pick up Baudrillard and Morrison the way my mother plunked at keys on the piano—reading from each marked page, picking out a rhythm. The seminar room was miles distant from Pieri's office, years away, too, and far grander even without a fireplace. Sometimes during break in the middle of class, Nobal would make us tea in the English Department office, taking orders on the corner of her legal pad, returning with a motley assortment of mugs.

When Toni Morrison published Love, Nobal began one particularly memorable lecture, *commercial culture was soaring. TV was taking off in earnest. The World Wide Web, too. Images were circulating in a big* 18 *way, produced cheaper, faster, than ever before.* She picked up a copy of *Seventeen* and waved it at us.

Now, there's a school of thought, she said, *that equates visual representation with liberation on a one-to-one basis.* Nobal pointed to *Love,* lying open against the table.

But Morrison challenges the idea that representation, even of the self, necessarily leads to power or freedom or safety.

Nobal was emphatic, waving her arms. I scribbled down notes: "...production of products <u>AND</u> images."

My Mother on Film

So that brings us to a big question Morrison addresses here. She paused, and we held our breath with her. *What happens when you lose control of your own image?*

That last line still echoes. What did Nobal *mean* by "your own image?" A photograph of you? A photograph you *take*? Other people's idea of who you are? Your memory?

In defeat, I have decided that "your own image" can be many things.

I have lost control of many things.

The month after our chat with Pieri, my mother was diagnosed with stage four lymphoma. The doctor told her she had four months to live, that she'd be dead before my fifteenth birthday. She relayed the news to me at the kitchen table, calmly, no tears. At risk for spillage, I packed my insides tightly together and stayed perfectly still while she talked.

My mother peeked into my room later that afternoon with two sheets of paper in her hand, a pro-and-con T-chart on each one. She sat on my bed and tucked a piece of hair behind my ear.

Pro of living with Uncle Colin, she said, *is that he will always have chocolate.* (My Uncle Colin was very fat.) *Con is that he farts like a garbage truck.*

I laughed in spite of myself. It made her eyes get shiny.

Sylvia will take good care of you, though. Mama said, all serious. *My brother married a good woman.* That hovered in the air for a moment. She took out the second sheet of paper.

Pro of living with Grandma is that you'll watch lots of Seinfeld.

Con, I said, *is that she might die, too.*

My other favorite Nobal lecture was also, oddly, about images. It was toward the end of the year, when the class was steeped in that familiar spring feeling of camaraderie and comfort. The semester was almost over, the stakes were lower, and at Nobal's seminar table at least, we found ourselves thrilled by each other's ideas and high on our own creativity. The discussions naturally sloped toward art by the end of the afternoon. Nobal, being Nobal, leaned into it. On

19

Natacha Markov-Ries

a Thursday in early May, she came prepared with a lecture on André Bazin, her notes again handwritten.

Why did the ancient Egyptians turn their dead into mummies? She always started with a bang. I don't remember our answers; somehow only Nobal's words stuck.

Bazin writes that in ancient cultures, people made art in order to defend against the passage of time. Mummification, but also painting and sculpture.

She glanced up and said the next sentence slowly, looking out over her glasses at us: *by preserving an image of corporeality, art satisfies a basic psychological need. To maintain bodily appearance in the face of death.*

Pencils moved across Moleskines.

That's why the Egyptians made terracotta statuettes, why Louis XIV wanted a portrait by Le Brün. Preservation of life through representation of life. Simple as that.

When my mother had only two months to live, I ordered a surveillance camera online. It came a week later, in an unmarked box. *What's that?* Standing at the sink, my mother shook clumps of suds off her hands. They dropped into the basin. Lifeless, easy, not a drop of fight.

It's a present, I told her. *For me.*

Oooh, elusive. My mother's eyes were glazed over, a blind woman's. She was gone— done—already. Her body looked frail against the steadiness of the counter, as she leaned over to scrub the decrepit pot, torso propped up like a paper doll, elbow high in the air for leverage. Frail. It was the first time I had ever used that word to describe my mother.

After she went to bed, I placed the surveillance camera on the windowsill over the sink, behind the knobby bonsai tree. It was the size of my palm, the camera, a smooth black square with a deep lens embedded in its cycloptic face. Nearly invisible against the dark marble of the countertop, you couldn't even tell when the little thing was on. I left the camera on for nine whole weeks, and turned it off only after my mother left the kitchen for the very last time.

★

Later on in the Bazin lecture, Professor Nobal reached into her bag and took out an old Kodak. The camera was boxy and silver—futuristic in that ancient *Star Trek* way.

Bazin claims that the advent of the camera changed everything, she told us. *Here, pass it around.* Nobal handed the camera to the boy on her left.

Photography finally satisfied our obsession with realism, she went on. *If the human endeavor is to preserve life by preserving an image of the deceased, then the camera is progress! Finally, mechanical reproduction!*

We sat, rapt. Nobal was wearing a dark velvet shirt and magenta glasses, her whole body radiating purple. I was especially captivated by her eyes—awed by their focus, moved by their warmth.

There's no room for human error in photography, Nobal said, *the way there is in painting or drawing. Or, I guess, in mummifying.* We laughed, eager to demonstrate our grasp of the joke.

Photos are perfect illusions, Nobal told us as our laughter quieted. *More than mere approximations. Bazin would tell us that the photographic image is the object itself, "freed from the conditions of time and space that govern it." Like I said, if we're talking about a psychological need to maintain bodily appearance in the face of death, well, people, photography is it.*

After my mother died, I went to live with Uncle Colin. He and Sylvia were incredibly generous. We often walked together in the woods behind their house. On the weekends they cooked elaborate lunches. Sylvia drew up little menus and we pretended their dining room was a restaurant.

"Will you be taking the check?" Colin would say at the end. I'd laugh. It was funny. Minutes later, my stomach would feel like a gaping mouth.

Sylvia gave me a journal, "for my thoughts." Colin dropped me off at the high school each morning and picked me up in the afternoon, so I wouldn't have to take the bus.

But every day after dinner, I'd go to my room (the guest room) and lock the door, glad to be alone. I'd lie flat on my stomach with my head to the side, pressed against the bed 'til my neck tightened and my shoulders ached. And I would rewatch the surveillance

Natasha Markov-Ries

footage from my kitchen at home. In chronological order, every moment.

There is my mother. She's frying eggs in the bright light of the morning, wearing pajama pants and a t-shirt she got free from the Farmer's Market. It says "I Tomato My Farmer," and has a big red tomato on the front, instead of a heart. She reaches up, opens the cabinet to the left of the stove, brings down a plate, picks up the pan, scoops out its sunny mounds. Here she is now, scraping the bottom of the pan with her spatula for the crispy ends. She puts the tip of the spatula in her mouth and grabs the eggy-bits with her teeth.

Cinema, Professor Nobal said, putting the old Kodak back in her bag at the end of the lecture, *goes even further than photography. It preserves the image of something in its duration.* At the bottom of my notebook, I wrote: "cinema—image in duration," and leaned back in my chair until I hit the bookshelves behind me. It was late, and my temple pulsed with exhaustion. Still, her next line jolted me:
  Bazin called cinema "objectivity in time." And really, that's exactly what movies are. They mummify change. Embalm time. Defer death. That's what she said. Movies defer death.

My memory of high school in Colin and Sylvia's home has mostly blurred away—the way windshield wipers sweep raindrops, back and forth, until no water is left. Even the security camera footage has become a summarized version of itself. A color here, a movement there. Except for the scene of my mother and Sylvia. That footage plays itself, over and over.

It is 2 a.m. and there is my mother, walking softly into the kitchen, turning on the light. My mother, with her thin arms, in her thin nightgown, sweeping her thinning hair behind her ears and grimacing at her reflection in the window. It is 2 am, and there is my mother, dying in the kitchen.
  The backdoor bangs shut. There is Sylvia, in the doorway to the kitchen. It's 2 a.m., and Sylvia is entering the kitchen. My mother

walks over to her, and Sylvia gathers my mother up, lifts her whole being into the air. My tendons are taut like Ms. Pieri's, they are snapping like Ms. Pieri's. My mother is snapping my tendons the same way she snapped Ms. Pieri's. And she is kissing Sylvia. My mother is kissing Sylvia, and Sylvia is kissing her.

A painter, right then, could have lifted his brush.

Sylvia and Colin took me out to dinner for my high school graduation. A grand affair: dark lighting, white napkins, a limited menu of specialties. They offered me wine, and I drank it despite the bitterness. It felt nice to get tipsy together. Talk inched, as it always did, toward my mother. How proud she would be. No more skipping school, an esteemed liberal arts college in my future.

Maybe I'll re-watch the footage, I murmured.

Colin furrowed his brow. *What footage?*

Eating good food with two people who loved me, made suddenly older by my glass of wine, I had let my secret slip. I was months away from leaving Oregon for New York and childhood no longer felt endless. So in a moment of stupidity or carelessness or trust, I explained how I had ordered the security camera and set it up in the kitchen. I didn't mention the scene of Sylvia and my mother, of course, but I saw realization inch into her eyes.

You ran the camera straight for the full two months?

Yes.

She covered her mouth with her hand. She excused herself to the bathroom.

Nobal asked, years later: What happens when you lose control of your image? What happens when control is wrested from you, by the grieving, greedy eyes of your own little girl?

Tipsy on the eve of my thirty-first birthday, I climb to the top of the staircase and lean way out over the railing with my big Canon camera. I am trying to capture the party below—the balloons and my beautiful, twirling friends.

Enough, my husband says, *with your fucking images.*

Natacha Markov-Ries

He's smiling, but there's a shard of truth in his words. Tired, I suppose, of my various preoccupations. I often make him watch Agnés Varda 21st century films, as I am convinced that her later work (while generally inferior to her earlier stuff) reflects an appropriate preoccupation with the slippery photo.

We laugh, of course, but in the silent space that comes after the talk, I grieve my mother's voice, my college years, and the look in Professor Nobal's eyes as she gives a question its full consideration. I never told my husband about Sylvia and my mother, or about the lecture that named me a thief. I don't want to make the moments into muted stories, to funnel feelings through awkward little words. Mostly, though, I don't want to let him reconstruct the scenes in his mind's eye. *My* images, so fearfully, so futilely, controlled. Then again, that is not her on my screen. Bazin is wrong. I want to return to the seminar room, to yell it at Professor Nobal as she hands me my tea. *André Bazin is wrong about everything.* And also: *I miss my mother in the kitchen. I miss my mother in every place.*

Andy Richter's Life in Quarantine

WYNNE HUNGERFORD

The sidekick becomes the star of his own self-isolation. Things are fine for a while, because for a while they are fine. He orders sushi and collects it at the door with gloves and a mask. He wears the same t-shirt for three days in a row and then takes an hour-long shower before FaceTiming with his manager, who says, "The business is fucked, but at least you've got a podcast." The business is a stuck pig. The blood is in the streets. The streets are empty. Smog lifts. He makes all of the brownie mixes in the pantry one afternoon, without regard for expiration date, and while he's busy cracking eggs and setting timers he longs for a marriage without an expiration date. Maybe next time, he thinks. When his children FaceTime him from their mother's house, he holds up a pan of brownies and jokes, "Anybody hungry?" and with voices as thin and hard as piano wire, they say, "Hey, Dad." They are burdened by their security, feeling trapped and bored and lost, even though the wonders of the known world are fulfilled by Amazon and delivered at their feet, those precious feet, so clean and narrow and soft, and in truth he wouldn't have it any other way. He thinks of how they were before Spotify took hold of them and the earbuds went in, his boy and his girl, his own flesh and blood, laughing and wiggling under the covers all those years ago, when this little piggy went to the market and this little piggy stayed home. They could not disappoint him, no, never, he loves them too much, but still the call ends with disappointment. If this crisis doesn't bring them back to calling him "Daddy" then nothing ever will. There is an assumption that the passage of time brings progress and that change means growth. He chose a long time ago to believe that those assumptions are true, because otherwise life would be a painful doggy paddle from one doomsday to the next and he would not be able to keep swimming. Medication helps. The walnuts in the brownies are stale, but he doesn't mind. It was expected and somehow welcome. His teeth are packed with walnuts and the sky is full of stars, even if they are mostly hidden. It's the presence of others that throws his own life into relief and without them, these people entering and exiting, on cue and of their own volition, he becomes the star of a one-man show, flickering, fading, losing heat. He has always known this about himself but now, being alone in the pandemic, in what people call, via email and text, "these crazy times," he's reminded that he's at his best with others. He doesn't just need people, he wants them in his life. What a gift, he thinks. What we've had and what we've been able to build. The sun slinks west and tender light fills the house and makes the walls look like suede. There is no one to turn to, no hand to gently squeeze. It's the symbol of the moon he misses, always just over his shoulder on the Conan set. Seeing that moon in his periphery was almost like catching a glimpse of himself in a mirror, something glowing, something round, something mundane yet magical, familiar yet unknown, always orbiting a celebrity planet. He was born to play the sidekick and he's grateful for it. Why be ashamed? A therapist once said, "It seems like you try very hard to say all the right things," and he denied it, of course, all the while being unaware of his denial, and the therapist said, "You want to mean it so badly, son, that it hurts." Love grows. Gratitude grows. Understanding expands. The common, human hurt is a pebble passed from shoe to shoe. He gets the idea of rearranging the furniture in his living room so that when he sits on the couch, he can see the moon over his shoulder, the real moon, through the sliding glass doors that lead to the backyard. It works. He sits down and sees the moon out of the

Andy Richter's Life in Quarantine

corner of his eye. Something's not right, though. He grabs a blazer from his closet and sits down again. That's better. Then the dog jumps into the armchair, upright and panting, a consummate late-night talk show host. The dog barks and he thinks, This is not the worst monologue I've ever heard. The audience applauds, though it's really the sound of his tinnitus, the collective drone of every crowd he's ever worked, and he pretends to catch the eye of a producer in the shadows, who gestures that it's time for a commercial break. The dog lets out a silent fart and he, Andy, Andy Richter, leans toward an imaginary guest sitting on the couch beside him. He imagines placing a friendly hand on the guest's shoulder or perhaps shaking their hand. He brings his mouth close to the guest's ear, quickly now, because the clock is ticking and they'll be live again soon, and this is what he loves, the momentary ascension into his best self, when he becomes warm, inquisitive, and complementary in every way, integral but not central, generous but not demanding, and though this window may be brief, he cannot help the ambition of his humanity. He asks, "Where do you come from, where are you going, and what have you learned?"

Wynne Hungerford

The Last Photograph of Tiny Tim

WYNNE HUNGERFORD

He's in a casket with his ukulele. He looks good. He looks dead, but he looks good. I showed it to some people. One person said, "Jesus," and another said, "He looks happy!" The heart attack that finally killed him occurred while he was singing "Tiptoe Through The Tulips" at a gala in Minneapolis. I've never been to Minneapolis, so I can't imagine what it even looks like there or what he might have looked like, unconscious, sweating, buttons pulling on his shirt, wife patting his cheeks, her breath dewy on his face, his breath barely there, barely, and then gone, but still the human smell coming from his open mouth, his spirit trying to escape in between bouts of CPR, rising through the clear (?) Minnesota sky, the EMS workers lifting him, heaving, pushing him into the back of the ambulance and taking him to die in the night, bringing him to it, right to the edge, and then watching him go over. Or I can imagine it. I was in a bad situation once. I'd gotten in a car accident with a man on a motorcycle. I wasn't on the motorcycle. He was on the motorcycle and I was in an SUV. My window turned bright blue the second before it shattered, the color of a swimming pool. The whole event was like a swimming pool. I had to swim through it, the beginning, middle, and end, before I could reach the other side and return to solid ground. The truth? When I heard him moaning in the road, I was relieved because my ability to hear meant that I was still alive and him moaning meant that he was still alive, and then when the ambulance took him away first, this young man, this boy, I had the most terrifying thought of my life, which was that he was not dead yet, but that he could die at any moment on the way to the hospital, and I almost said, "Bring him back, please bring him back, because if you take him away, I won't know if the moaning stops." There are things I can't talk about now, except that my injuries were fixed with rods and screws and I still consider myself unscathed. The tightening of hardware tightens the guilt. When I was in high school, I once swam in a pool near a cemetery. Wind blew fake flowers onto the water. I pretended that I was in Hawaii and wore the flowers in my hair. I felt beautiful then. There was blood on the glass, I remember that much. The glass was stained but it wasn't stained glass. Christ and his crown of thorns, weeping from his wounds... I don't know when Tiny Tim actually died, if it was at the gala hosted by a women's club or if it was in the ambulance or if it was at the hospital. All I know is that his career had died a long time before his body died and he'd tried to revive it again and again. It wouldn't restart. His heart wouldn't restart. That's not all. On May 15, 1970, he and his first wife had a stillborn baby, which they named "It." There's a photograph of the headstone on www.findagrave.com. I was looking for another headstone when I stumbled upon that one. Someone even left digital flowers on this grave's webpage for the 50th anniversary of the baby's death. That particular user left a comment, saying, "As your father once said, One day IT will open the pearly gates for me. Rest easy little one for you are with your father in heaven." The name almost seems like a joke, but surely it couldn't have been a joke. If Tiny Tim had been a religious man, wouldn't he have worried that prayers going to "It," his son, his proper noun, might have gotten mixed up with all of the prayers for all of the other miscellaneous "its" of the world? "Let it be peaceful, Lord." "Let it be quick." My hair looks like Tiny Tim's. My teeth are also long and yellow. It's funny to have ever felt beautiful, even for an afternoon. If I had an open casket funeral and someone approached, I doubt they would say, "She looks happy!" and I doubt

29

Wynne Hungerford

they would take a photograph. I don't know what they'd say. I don't want to know. So far, online visitors have left 103 digital flowers for "It." There might be more as time goes on, but even if this is all there ever is, it still seems like a lot. I guess the downside with digital flowers is that you can't smell them and the upside is that they can't die. Here's something: I close my eyes and see Christ in all his modesty walking across that swimming pool by the cemetery, tiptoeing so as not to disturb the flowers.

The Last Photograph of Tiny Tim

Loo–Lah

NIAMH BAGNELL

I wake from nightmares—I was there and saved her or I was there and tried but couldn't save her, just watched it all in slow motion, frozen in horror. I wake and there's never that moment of forgetting I hear others talk about. It's the remembering that wakes me most days, wondering what could have been different.

It's frightening how quickly a six-pack collapses to flab. I've been sinking into sloth with the last half year, watching Friday night boxing matches from the couch, no longer a fighter myself, not bothering even with the local fights. So, I watch fellas far better than I'd ever been, strutting their muscle, making me sick. Mam's cat curled beside me most nights with an "I suppose you'll have to do" attitude, marmalade arse towards me. That particular Friday night, the cat was left alone, to rule over an empty house. I was in the factory, covering for the night cleaner.

Nights has advantages. Something soothing about starting at intake and working your way through the whole place. It's not huge, so one person can cover the lot. I'm not all proud, trying to do everything perfect, the way the usual fella goes on—I just enjoy the process. Taking big toys apart and putting them back like glistening silvered Lego. Giants, they split before me with metallic groans, showing their filth in secret places; places that were dark for the day, and too dangerous to enter. I forgive the day's sins of dirt, replacing them with all types of shiny.

The biggest plus is the lack of the boss-man. He smiles a crooked smile, almost gleeful, as he declares the work isn't good enough, pretending to be pals, one of the lads. He came to Mam's funeral with the same stupid smile. Told me to take as long as I want, just be sure to drop a text soon as possible, let him know when to expect me, he had to work out the rota. I swear, only the coffin was beside us.

He pulled me in for an awkward heart-to-heart in his hidey-hole office when I returned.

"Will you be alright, Murph," he lifted an eyebrow "after what happened? Not being insensitive, but you've had your issues too, haven't you?"

"What.. with Diago? That was just a bit of fun" Debbie, from HR way over-reacted, misunderstood the whole situation.

"Yes, well, in light of recent events," with a nervous laugh he waved at the door, "I want to be sure you're, like, stable. Keep the horse-play for boxing, yeah?" I focussed on his teeth as I nodded, thinking of shrapnel-ing them, a power shot leaving jagged clumps where they once sneered. I didn't tell him I don't box no more.

So, no boss-man. No other muppets either, talking too much or tip-toeing around me. Trying not to provoke my ire. A quiet one.

I realised, when I got there, I'd have company after all. The new girl, Sinead, had a mix on, her yellow labels plastered all over it. She'd surely arrive at some ungodly hour, to check on it. The things they make the graduates do. Her job's nearly as bad as mine. Nearly, but not quite. At least she has a hope of moving on from being factory fodder. She will eventually escape from being forever in white coats, wellies, goggles and gloves, washing hands like an obsessive compulsive, watching clocks like a gom, living always for the next break.

Knowing she'd be in, I felt lighter. I didn't know her well at the time, she was only in the door a few weeks, but I knew enough. She was different. When she'd been asked to be "the eyes", (something bosses get their young to do from early days, to drive home the fact that the workers aren't human, just something to be watched); she apologised for intruding, explained what she was looking for, mocked the absurdity of it with us.

"Hi Murph" she called out brightly over the power-washer roar, like we were at the beach, and she looking for a nice spot for her towel. I felt a bubble of mirth rise inside at the sight of her, and her happy-go-lucky swing. I waved a hand and turned back to my task, holding myself a little straighter than before, maybe something of the usual guy's attention to detail about me.

I heard an exclamation, like she was scolding the mix for misbehaving. The shouts continued, so I turned. Her hairnet was askew, her front soaked and she clutching a sample in one hand. The other hand frantic, trying to screw down the lid. Foam rioted over, torrential spilling down onto what *had* been my spotless floor. I felt a black scribble of electric anger, a college kid coming in and wrecking the place, bloody typical. I walked over, tapped the sides to settle the pot—shooing her off, didn't blink as it gushed at me, closed it.

"Never open the lid while a mix is on, don't ya see the tap?" I said, livid, despite myself.

"They said make sure and get some off the top." She looked comically nervous, and I softened, understanding the mistake.

"They never said about the lever?"

She looked where I nodded, at a bar that pushes the tap to the desired depth.

"Oh my god, I'm such a Loo-lah!"

She asked if I'd have to report it, and I enjoyed her earnest green   33
eyes, told her I wouldn't.

Maybe that was a mistake, letting her know I was soft on her. She'd likely heard from others what an asshole I could be about these things.

"Such a Loo-lah!" I repeated to myself, driving home through the summer's dawn after that first close encounter, as little rabbits scuttered off by-roads in my way. I couldn't stop, it made me laugh, so I kept it up "Such a Loo-lah!"

Niamh Bagnell

★

She thanked me again shortly after, joked she'd thought I'd actually kill her, with my thunder face.

"Ah sure, nine years in a place, you know what's what." I saw her calculating, "Obviously starting work aged eleven was tough—" Her laugh was a fizz in my gut, an explosion of joy.

In the weeks that followed she kept finding excuses to talk. Maybe she was just as friendly with everyone but it felt focussed.

This at a time when most people shunned me, awkwardness had become a habit. People still not knowing what to say. The canteen quietening, just a smidge, when I'd walk in. Others wanting details, prying, asking if I'd seen it coming, morbidly thrilled with their access to my almost first-hand account. Some of them probably convinced it was me that did it, that Dad took the fall, admitted manslaughter so I'd go free. I'd been questioned alright, which probably seeded the rumour, but wasn't ever seriously suspected, I think.

She said I was the nicest person on the floor. "The floor" from her sounded honourable, a place where magic might happen, the very edge of everything that mattered. Really the place was never that important to me, a means to an end. Money for shiny shorts, protein powders, everything geared for my glory future as a pro, at least in the long ago. I kept waiting for an end, she would grow distant. It never came. Her eyes lingered on mine. She laughed when I told her my Dad said the phrase "green-eyed monster" was about green-eyed people being mad, rather than jealous, because of how much their eyes changed colour.

I even admitted he was talking about Mam, whose eyes changed with her mood—from fiery iridescence to soft mossy-grey. He also said he never knew which version he'd wake up to 'til she opened her eyes each morning. I didn't tell Sinead how he joked he'd never need to stray since she was so many different women at once. Mam's eyes narrowed when he said that and he'd shut up quick. There was always a little snarl at the edge of their jokes, a bite to their laughter, even on good days.

Loo-Lah

It felt like friendship, with Sinead. I'd see her coming and know it'd be easy. I liked to pretend to explain things to her, obvious things, just for fun. She'd laugh at anything, even jokes about her housemate, HR Debbie.

Of course, going further crossed my mind, and the possible problems that might ensue but then I reasoned, no, she saw me as an older brother. This freed me from over-thinking. The friendly fizz-making banter continued with no reason in the world to stop.

This Friday there was a going away. Away back to Lithuania with one of the lads. I don't usually go out, but I hadn't any food in the house and knew there'd be chips. So, even though it's a dingy little hole, I walked over to the local, where the whole factory had gathered after work.

Debbie shot daggers when I walked in, while Sinead looked glad to see me. They were very done up. Her dress was like underwear, a coloured material with black lace. I stood in a dark corner, letting the leery nonsense of the lads from "the floor" drift round me, the boss-man even put in an appearance to buy a round, slapping lads on the back. An '80s mix played off someone's phone on speakers, the bright happy music clashing loudly with dark wood and plain furnishings. She kept looking over, laughing, mouthing lyrics at me. Debbie kept trying to pull her back to their drunken dance.

The party ended with half the factory back at their place, in the new estate in the village, the very centre of nowhere, a handy spot. It was all inspirational posters, cake pictures, an Eiffel Tower clock; Debbie's taste.

Diago squared himself up at me in the hallway. "Are you ever coming back for a few rounds Murph?" the first time in six months he'd said anything remotely banter-like to me, since before. He mimed a one-two punch. A lull fell in the chatter around me. "I miss having something soft to play with," he added.

I pointed between his legs, "You could play with that" I said, and people laughed a 'glad there won't be a fight' laugh because that would've been our usual form but Diago was laughing too, knew

Niamh Bagnell

he'd walked into that one. Maybe he'd handed it to me on purpose.

I went to the kitchen, the reminder of boxing had sunk me.

"How are ye Murph?" her soft voice found me peering into the ginormous fridge, curious about what they'd have—loads of light beer, wilted salads, cheese.

"Oh, I'm fine, just fine." We began chatting as always, she soon had me laughing like during the day, but everything closer. Her hand resting on my arm as she smiled, or moving to put her mouth beside my ear so I could hear her better, though the music wasn't that loud.

Debbie came out and asked was she alright, and she said she was fine thanks. They stared at each other a few seconds. The boss-man faltered in the door soon after Debbie, making out he was looking for a bottle-opener. I thought how very sharply-cut HR Debbie is, and how perfectly she'd go with the boss-man, and his shrapnel teeth.

"Time for a tour!" Sinead whisked me out the back where we surveyed colleagues smoking, shifting, singing into darkness.

She led me upstairs, encouraged me to try her bed. She joined me, and I had no thoughts…of why, or whether she really wanted me, only kissed her back, enjoying the feel of her silly shiny clothes and her firm body underneath. She stopped it at underwear, and fell asleep too quickly, leaving me crawling with desire, giddy head wondering if she was being cruel on purpose, maybe this was part of the game, maybe I had to wake her, sweep her reluctance aside. I told myself not to be stupid, not to confirm anyone's bad opinion of me. Instead I ground my desire down to nothing beneath myself and then fell hard into my own drunken sleep.

36

She woke me early in the morning, wanting to drive up the "mountains", see autumn colours, like tourists.

We walked back to the factory to pick up my car, getting orange juice on the way in the shop half of the local pub for breakfast. Casual, like nothing happened. Like I had nothing to do this Saturday and we were just friends, hanging out.

Loo-Lah

I told her as we drove, just to break the silence, how Mam once dragged my Dad up this way for a hike.

"Like water, falling, how bloody exciting," he'd laughed as he told about it, years ago, an example of why never to follow a woman's interests. "It was miserable when we finally found it," he'd remembered, "more like your granny's shower, just a dribble, no pressure."

"You just never look at things the right way," Mam said at the time. "I don't know why I thought you'd see it."

I didn't suggest we follow in their footsteps, told her they only visited the once.

"Just the once?" She mused. "They mustn't have thought much of it."

We reached a scenic car park and stood out for a view, a low wall guarded a sheer drop. Those so-called mountains are really only hills but the sky stretched wide and busy with morning colour.

"Murph, what are your dreams?"

"That's when you see films but only in your head, when you're asleep and you completely forget them when you wake, mostly."

She laughed. "No, I mean what do you care about?"

"Big question."

"I know" she said. "It's just—I'm fairly sure mine don't involve making rich people richer." She sat onto the low wall, looking out over the view. "But then my parents want me safe and sensible, so I stay in the steady job, on the career ladder, to keep up the illusion that I listen."

She went quiet, the hills hushed too, no traffic, nothing disturbing the wide-open silence.

"I wondered what yours were."

"Well, I haven't given it much thought." Disappointment sank her expectant face. We sat in silence for a few seconds. I looked at my hands make fists and stretch out the fingers again. Thinking about padded gloves, the roar of the crowd and the shine of the trophies. It's all a world away, knocked out of my life in a flash, as if

Niamh Bagnall

all the power trickled away impossibly with the news of what had happened at home.

I've met Dad only once since, in the brightly-lit room for visitors, pale hands knotted on a metal table, pleading.

"I didn't mean it," he pulled at his own ear, "It was a complete accident. She pushed too hard, you know that, with years she pushed, and I mean I—"

His voice leaden with regret.

"I caught her wrong—"

All the talk of discipline, awareness of your power, respecting it, using it only in the right context. How boxing had saved him from his tough beginnings, given him a release, a chance to shine.

I stood and asked the guard to let me out.

As I stared into my hands, Sinead whispered her worries at me. All the safe little worries of a standard bubble-dwelling twenty-something-year-old: home, the farm, the dog she misses that's getting lame, the parents she'd never please, how she worries sometimes what the boss-man thinks. Why she whispered, only she knew, maybe to try and keep me close. Maybe thought I'd run off if she doesn't keep the intrigue going. I was glad that she stopped things the night before, making what I had to do easier.

Her hand was on mine and she leant towards me, seeking a kiss, our first one sober.

"I'm sorry Sinead."

"You didn't do anything…yet" she grinned.

"I can't."

"Oh." She looked away, at the hills, the empty road, squinted. "Well…I can't force you." But her lovely eyes returned, questioning and hurt welling into liquid depth. I realised how easily she could force me, how I'd do anything for her if she got a proper hold.

I panicked to get away, to guarantee our freedom, I moved back to the car alone. She followed, haltingly, puzzled. When she got in, I drove down to shelter and a narrowing sky. I thought how much better that we ride along stewing in silence, punctuated by the odd

Loo-Lah

sniff, than if I had tried to fool us both into thinking we could be together.

Later I get curry, tell myself it's alright. I can worship from afar, without being too close. "HR Debbie can't fire me for being an asshole, can she?" I ask the marmalade cat. Its eyes seem momentarily to ponder my words, they slowly blink, and look away. I realise the animal is lost in its own concerns.

Monday, Diago and I are on the packing line when she comes to do a trial along with the boss-man, lighter caps, for the environment. She addresses herself nervously to Diago to start the line again when she has loaded them up. He puts it running and it doesn't work. Something jams, but the line keeps pushing, so bottles get crushed at an awful speed and fall, gushing product all over the floor, a maniacal crunching sound marking each cycle. I dive on the red stop button and there's silence. We begin to gather the wasted bottles into crates. Diago throwing them into the crate that I hold.

Boss-man puts on his nastiest face, half amused but vicious he takes out his phone to call for maintenance. Sinead finally meets my eye, as he's telling them that 'Bambi' has done it again. "Yeah," he says, "I fuckin' know."

He starts to walk away and my gloved hands tighten on the crate. It's heavy with the spewing half-full bottles. I lift and throw it through the air, satisfied with the strength I find in my arms. I didn't mean it to hit him, not really. It catches his shoulder and he goes down. The surprised look on his crooked face makes me want to laugh. Lads making boxes stop what they're doing to stare.

"Suppose you're happy now!" I say to her, though I know it makes no sense, her wide eyes are the colour of spring. There's a wetness on my face and I remind myself so much of my Dad I almost expect to see him, somewhere crouched among the boxes. The boss-man struggles to his feet and clutching at his arm, backs away towards the door. I follow, tearing off my factory coat and hairnet as I go.

Asian—Asian

JAMES MORENA

The Filipino boy, maybe ten, mahogany skin, disheveled yellow tank top and green corduroy pants, tight-fisted the wire fencing that made up the rickety, oval cockpit. The two-foot-high fence, zip-tied together, snagged his shirt or gripped his jeans as he bobbed and weaved along with his Kelso. Feathers exploded, then fluttered from—and lingered in—the air. Squawks and crows sliced yells and hoots. Slaps and smacks reverberated off threadbare t-shirts and light, summer jackets.

It had felt wrong seeing some child here, after midnight, watching a cockfight in an abandoned downtown building sticky with Mexican beer and American smokes, and even more fucked having that same snot-nose in the front row while me and these birdrats bobbed and weaved in the back rows just to catch a glimpse of the roosters' slashing middle toes, jabbing beaks, and clumsy flapping and flying about 'til death—theirs or their opponents'—ended their one-time service.

The Asian bro, maybe Malaysian, Thai, Vietnamese, next to me was no help when I asked, "Who's that kid?" The guy, pointing into the crowd, said in a thick accent something I couldn't make out.

"That boy there," I said, also pointing.

"Yes," the guy said.

"Yes, what?" I looked at his smiling, almond-shaped eyes. "That boy. That boy. Him."

"Yes," the guy awarded me with two thumbs up, then turned to the man beside him and said something funny. The other man craned to look at me, then laughed at the joke.

I called the kid Tukoy because I have a cousin on my mother's side, my Filipino side, with that name, and I have always wanted to call someone by that name. So I said, "Tukoy," to no one. Later when the fight started, I noticed tears flowing down Tukoy's bony cheeks, accentuating the grooves and divots below his eyes and next to his nostrils.

Some former bartender of the Austin, live-music venue we loitered in had organized tonight's fight. "Ain't nobody 'bout to know," the dude word-of-mouthed for a month prior, since the joint—and pizza and ma and pop's and bowling alleys—had shut down. The dude too had set the rules: fifteen minutes of blood-sporting, fifteen minute break, then another round. One minute before the match, though, there'll be observations—the rooster's size, his aggressiveness, human's bullshitting and shit talking—then two minutes of stakes and claims, minimum $200 buy in, before the battlers waylaid, and spit and sweat splashed from spectators' lips and brows.

Word meandered through the crowd when betting had opened:

"The boy own the rooster," someone said.

"We're using the kid's pet?" I asked.

"It Kelso," a co-worker informed me.

"What's that?" I asked.

"It has world class lineage," a gambler across from us said.

No one replied to me. Bullshit was everywhere.

I had never seen a cockfight before, but some of my Asian co-workers—they cooked the ramen, I delivered their creations—had claimed: "You're white-Asian, not Asian-Asian," because I had yet to attend an event. But I wanted to be more Asian-Asian so I hopped a ride with a group of them to the fight and to my full-Asian-ness.

Someone shouted, "The betting stops in thirty seconds."

James Morena

I looked about the room. Tried to gauge who to bet on. Is it bad luck to bet on a child's pet? Is it good luck because it must have been cared for? Loved?

I imagined Tukoy dancing around the chicken coop when his Kelso was laid. I imagined Tukoy squealing and laughing at the large brown egg popping out of the "chicken's ass." I imagined Tukoy cradling the egg, hiding it in his laundry basket to keep it warm, then helping to peel away the shell after the chick, his Kelso, had pecked pecked fought its way into Tukoy's spindly arms. I could see Tukoy playing hide and seek moments after Kelso had imprinted Tukoy as its mother. Tukoy and Kelso jogged and sprinted with and away from each other. They scaled mounds of dirt, then huge hills. Tukoy and Kelso ate from the same dinner plate. They were insep-arable. I saw in my mind Tukoy saying, "I love you, Kelso." Then as Kelso grew, the roles changed as the gamecock protected Tukoy from other roosters, from dogs, and from Tukoy's five siblings. Kelso proved to be strong and determined, then valuable and absolutely necessary in the pits.

Before the timer had buzzed, I threw down $1500 in cash. My co-workers had said to bet like an Asian-Asian, which meant big even if I didn't have the money to waste.

I said, "I am Asian-Asian," as I watched some bookie scoop my bet, then disappear into the crowd.

The bartender, now match ref, snatched Kelso from Tukoy's arms when the time came. The dude paraded Kelso for the onlookers, holding him in both hands—arms extended straight out then overhead, then straight again. Smoke thickened and blued the air. Heat emanated off the heads and backs of the now crazed bystanders. The bartender made two laps around the pit. I noticed each time he came full circle Kelso and Tukoy stared into each other's eyes. Parent and child, mother and chick.

Two dudes let loose the roosters. A detonation of feathers and screams and fist pumps. Grown men shoved each other. Cigarettes dangled from mouths. Everyone except the front row prairie dogged for better views. Tukoy remained still and straight-faced when the bout started. His hands dangled at his sides. He stood pigeon-toed.

I kept my eyes on the kid. His winces. His recoils. His surrender to the wire fence. His hands looked so small. He looked even smaller. When Tukoy's chin fell to his chest, I began to cry along with him. I whispered, "Kelso." Tears trickled down my cheeks because I knew that my rent money had been lost and that my co-workers would finally deem me an Asian-Asian.

James Morena

At the Same Time

MELISSA SHARPE

I am making tea. I get the biggest mug I have, fill it nearly to the top with tap water, microwave it for one minute and thirty seconds, and then I'll try this new jasmine green tea. I am making tea. The crackly buzzer by my door growls at me. I already know it's Phillip. I can't even think of who else both knows that I live here now *and* would even want to visit me. I walk over to the door and push the button as far in as it will go, yelling, "What?"

"Let me in. I left my keys."

"That's your fault."

"Just walk down the stairs and unlock the door for me, man."

This stupid eight-unit building. There were six other people I could have ended up across the hall from. Six other people I could share a rear balcony with. I go down the stairs and open the front door. Here I am in the dark. In this old building, letting in my irresponsible neighbor. You can hardly believe I was making a seventh birthday cake not that long ago. In a totally new and bright white kitchen. Apron around my waist, I swear. But I don't get to do that anymore. That was back when I lived in the townhouse. The tiles on the floor of this apartment are original to the building.

Phillip has a bottle of something in a crunchy paper bag clenched in one fist. He holds it up and gives it a gentle sway back and forth. It's so late, and the day won't end. I try to let Phillip walk up the stairs first, but he just stands there, so I go up first.

I picked this apartment because I could afford it, and I thought the neighborhood was one of those places where everyone was relaxed and painted outdoors on the weekends or something. I don't know. It felt like something that would make sense because there was a yoga studio not too far away, and not that I was going to do yoga, but that was the type of mood I needed to be around. Some kindness. A place where everyone would love to be a part of me starting over or whatever I was doing.

My microwave beeps once. A reminder that I have to come get something out of it.

True story: I took that microwave from the basement of Michael's townhouse.

At Michael's townhouse, when I lived there, the neighbors never left their keys behind or annoyed me. If anyone was wondering.

Phillip tugs the bottle out of the paper bag to reveal that it was, in fact, a bottle of rum. That isn't annoying, but Phillip is always irritating me in other ways. See it's so easy to end up at his apartment because of the balcony we share. You go out there, and then he's out there with his friends, and then you look around and it's like you are doing something. Look at me! I'm with all these people. I can have so much fun! I want to record it. I take pictures. Try to make Phillip and his friends look older. My age or close to it. So fun, right? I have to press my finger to the circle on my phone screen twice before it takes the picture.

That party on the balcony could be my new life, and if I try, maybe I can make you wish it was yours. And you sure as shit don't want it.

When I was still at Michael's townhouse, one day his phone was on the table next to me, and it kept humming and humming. I could glance to the side and see the partial messages on the center of his screen. Buzz: She wasn't happy. Buzz: What was he thinking? Buzz: So much more to consider. Even with that humming and buzzing around me, I enjoyed that life so much I forgot to take pictures of it.

Melissa Sharpe

There is a slight chance that because we have spent a lot of nights on the balcony talking and drinking, and because we have gone grocery shopping together twice, and sometimes I do borrow or lend him things, that Phillip believes we are friends. But I hate the sight of him. He's easily fifteen years younger than me, and he wears shirts with dumb things on them like flames.

On the balcony, Phillip opens a beer and hands it to a friend of his, a guy I have seen before and perhaps have met, but still he seems unfamiliar. When I can't remember people and things, I make deals. Once I can't remember X number of things, I know it is time for me to start doing *this* so I can remember better. Or stop doing *this other thing*, so I can remember better. If I lose my keys, I won't drink for a week. That sort of thing.

I had this glass Phillip handed me, but for some reason I can't find it, so I go in my apartment to get a new one. It's not a bad place, really, I have this air plant hanging above the sink. It is my second air plant. With the first one, I thought you didn't have to do anything to it and it grows. Just grows. No water, no soil, it survives on the air. As it turns out, interestingly enough, you have to water your air plant pretty regularly. But without anything under it to catch the water, you have to put them in your sink to soak or spray them. It's about 7,000 times more inconvenient than a regular old house plant. But because I killed the first one, and I know you don't get to try many things over again, I'm taking care of this air plant and giving it a bath in the sink every week.

At Michael's townhouse, which I used to live in, he had all these house plants. So much greenery and lushness. In the dining room there was a tree. A goddamn tree. A ficas, with these brilliant medium-green leaves and gentle twisty branches. It was cultivated love. But it was also so much decay. The wet soil always smelled like someone's disease, and the leaves would curl and rot as they fell in the pot and all over the floor. Michael would bake chicken with rosemary, but I couldn't tell if we were celebrating domesticity or eating flesh surrounded by decomposing plants.

After Michael, and Michael's townhouse, I found this apartment. Remember how I chose it because it was cheap? So cheap, in fact—

you'll love this—that it was mostly twenty-year-olds with room-mates who lived there. It was minutes from the college downtown, and all those bars nearby aren't bad.

I get my glass and fill it with ice and rum and a spoonful of vanilla ice cream. It's what someone who didn't like drinking would drink, so it gives me a chance to pretend that I am that type of person. I can't take a sip until I get on the balcony, see, because I don't drink alone. That was my resolution for this week. I have stuck to it. And once I forget two more things then I'll stop drinking on Fridays altogether.

Tonight, however, I only forgot one guy who I maybe didn't even know. Also, I'm not drinking alone now. I'm drinking on my balcony with my neighbor and his friends. I'm okay for right now.

I forgot someone's birthday last week. I had remembered it weeks ago, made a mental note to buy a card, to find a gift, to bake a cake, to buy a cake, to do something. Then as the days tripped and stumbled along, I lost the note. Crumpled it in my brain. Got confused because the weather is much warmer for March than usual, so I thought maybe it was May. I forgot someone's birthday this week.

Juliana turned eight. A big, round set of circles. A double halo. A snowman. An infinity sign. Eight years, and I wasn't there even though I was there when she turned seven. She turned eight and I forgot. I remembered, briefly, early, when it didn't count. Then I forgot when it mattered.

When Juliana turned seven, I baked a cake. We baked it together. The mix was from a box, but we added the rest of the ingredients and stirred it, which as a child—hell, as an adult—is close enough to baking from scratch. We tipped the mixing bowl together to pour it into the cake pan.

See, we had plans for this cake. We had decorating supplies. We were going to do this the *real* way. We had to wait for the cake to cool, so Juliana listened to these songs she liked, and I had a glass of wine and read a magazine. Michael in the other room, asking how it was going.

When the cake had cooled, Juliana and I scooped frosting into bags with metal tips tucked in the ends and began to decorate the cake with puffy stars, shell-shaped lines, and whatever else the tips did for us as we squeezed. It's fun getting to see how your hands can change the outcome of the frosting. You can lick the extra off your finger.

Sometimes you don't have to remember all the details of a day because it is just like every other day. But a day where you bake a cake—you remember that day. What did we do the day after? I'm not sure. I think it was a Sunday, so Michael had to drop Juliana off with her mom. I don't know what we did, though. No clue. I think I had wanted us to go out to dinner and clean up. It was Michael's townhouse, I think I said that, but I lived there. So the day after Juliana's birthday I probably wanted to clean. I was thinking about birthdays and parties and fun and cake—I can't remember if Michael did anything like sigh or complain or roll his eyes or give me some sort of clue that he was going to break up with me the next week.

I take my glass outside. When Phillip looks at me, he lingers a bit and turns away. It's because we had kissed some time back. I was convinced I could do it. That it didn't matter that I was a licensed driver the year he was born. I could do it. I shouldn't have, though. Everything was buffed shiny and fun because we made margaritas with some guys he knew. We had these tacos. He placed his hands on my waist, under the shirt, and it felt like I had finally recovered. But we stumbled, too, and I think I said we shouldn't. And so we stopped. Right there in the hallway of our apartment building.

Phillip and his friends are playing a game where each person has to name an animal that begins with a letter of the alphabet. Someone starts with A, then the next person gets B, and so on until someone can't name an animal. Then they are out, or they have to take a drink, or nothing happens because they don't seem that concerned with the rules. After animals (ending with "zebra," obviously) they move on to movie titles. I get up to refill my glass because it's okay to have one drink per stupid game that your neighbor plays.

"Bring me one," this guy says. It's Phillip's other friend, who is more unrecognizable than the first.

"What?"

"Can I have one of those, too?" he asks. Pauses. "Please?"

"Yeah, sure."

Phillip's friend is named Glazier, which I don't believe until he shows me his license.

I also have a rule about making sure I go to bed before one in the morning, because for the love of everything, that is late enough to be up drinking with your neighbor's friends on the balcony.

Phillip and his friends will stay up later. They don't have rules yet because they are young and play drinking games and they haven't done anything complicated yet. They make great company for the evening—no matter who they are around—and then in the morning they feel okay, so they don't make rules yet.

One day at a science center, Juliana and I pulled on this rope with all our might. The rope was connected to a pulley up above, which then was connected to hundreds and hundreds and hundreds and hundreds of pounds of weight. If you stand on the first circle on the ground, it is pretty much impossible to pull down hard enough to life the weight. If you go to the second circle on the ground, some people may be able to lift the weight. If you stand at the third circle on the ground, you can totally pull the weight. The third circle is the farthest away and the plaque next to it explains that distancing yourself from the weighted load allows for the work required to lift it to be distributed. Backing away from the hard work makes it easier to do. Yet Juliana and I stood on the second circle pulling that rope as hard as we could. Stuttered laughs as we dangled off the ground. I could hear Michael that day, sort of far away but not really, whispering into a phone. These little phrases like, "I'm not talking about this now," and "She's fine. She's fine" popping out louder than the rest. I kept tugging on that rope; making the work hard by being so close.

I sit in one of the chairs on the balcony and sip. Phillip calls over to me. Some of them are going in his apartment to play cards. Do I want to join them? It's late, and I'm just going to go home—but thanks anyway. When I say it, it sounds like I live so far away. But really, I'm four feet away.

Melissa Sharpe

Last week I had these giant paper grocery bags, and they were hard to hold in my hands while unlocking my door. I put them on the floor, as you will, just as Phillip was coming out of his door. "Oh, hey, hi," he said, pulling a hand through his hair and closing the door behind him. "I can't help—I have to go," he said and went down the stairs two at a time. I didn't need help, though. It was three bags. They were on my floor, and in thirty seconds they would be inside with me. I would put the chicken where it goes, the crackers where they go, and I'd make sure the lettuce was front and center so I'd eat it before it wilted into a brown, unforgiving sludge. But I didn't need help with any of that. What did Phillip think was going on in my life?

On the balcony, Phillip's friends go into his apartment, but leave his door open. It's the end of the night I suppose; if only all things had such clear endings. Phillip and his friends are loud through his open door.

When I go inside, my apartment is blue with the glow of the TV. I have blinds that are made out of something pretending to be wood, and I spin the rod until they are shut as tight as they can go. I can still hear Phillip and his friends as if they are the noise of my apartment, too. I am fine with it tonight because I'm going to have the TV on, and that makes noise anyway. I'll sleep in a minute.

We used to play this game, Michael, Julianna, and myself. You would move around the board, and everyone would try to land on the same spot as your piece to knock you out. You'd be there, just moving around, following a path, and then *uh oh* someone landed where you were and you had to go all the back to start. You were completely innocent, minding your own business you know, and it was the other person that messed your shit up. I guess you could say it was your fault for playing with them in first place.

I want to find something on TV that is both interesting and that will put me to sleep. I can choose between enthusiastic people trying to sell me stuff and a cooking show. I go with the cooking show. This lady is flipping shrimp in a pan with paprika and something else. God I'm so lonely right now. She wilts spinach in the pan with the shrimp and promises me it will taste great over any grain I choose. Any! It's up to me!

One day at Michael's townhouse I was rinsing dishes off before putting them in the dishwasher. I washed, while Michael went outside because Juliana's mom showed up, and she was angry. Julianna had to stay in the car. "This is still our life, even though we aren't together, some things are *shared*. And you shouldn't add, subtract, or change it in any way without talking to me about it. You don't know what negative effect you can have. You have one thing, *one person,* to put first—and surprise! You failed. You failed, Michael."

I don't really like shrimp because I can never tell if it has been cooked properly or if someone took the time to remove the shit from their backs.

In the morning I have to make coffee. My coffeemaker is a piece. If I take the pot out before it is done brewing, the coffee spills everywhere. I open my door to the balcony to let the air in. It's cold, the way it should be this time of year. One of Phillip's friends is out there already. Or still out there. He doesn't see me look at him. None of these people are my friends. None of this is mine. I pour the coffee and look out my window at that friend of Phillip's. He is on the phone. Leaning over the railing.

Michael used to have these giant coffee cups, and we would fill them up twice some mornings. These foggy and slow weekend mornings, when it was just us, and I could stay there. Sometimes we would make eggs or something. If it was cold: watch a movie under a blanket. I bought new hand towels for the bathroom.

I was in the bathroom the first time I heard Juliana's mom call, screaming. I'm not sure how many times she called before, but this was the first one I could hear. Something was wrong because Michael told her to quiet down, but even when he walked a room away I could hear her explain that I didn't *matter at all.* It was, as I heard, *none of my business.*

And then all that time later when Michael broke up with me, I tried to ask him what I would do—I mean, really, what would I *do?* He said I would do what I had always done, which is the dumbest

Melissa Sharpe

shit he had ever said because we broke up and I'm not baking cakes and taking Juliana to the science center. I haven't put a pony tail in anyone else's hair or washed the dishes after a family meal. I'm not watering the houseplants of a man who told me one thing before telling me another. I'm not doing any of that shit, am I?

Mornings in the apartment used to feel like a new chance each day. Now the sun only highlights the dust in this place while trying, it really is trying, to nourish that air plant at the same time. Phillip comes out on the balcony and knocks on my door. I let him in. It is early and maybe he brought me breakfast. Only he is empty handed. "Maybe we should talk?" he says, but I don't have anything to say to him.

"I don't want to talk about anything. There can't be anything to say."

"I just think," he starts. Pulls a hand through his hair. "I don't want it to be weird or complicated now."

I laugh. I try to sound like a sophisticated woman on television. I should be sophisticated compared to him. "It's not weird. It's so not complicated," I say before taking a sip of coffee. My pot hisses. "Don't worry."

"Okay, I just, you know," he says. Phillip looks over his shoulder like he should leave, but maybe he should stay.

"I'm not going to be here much longer anyway," I say. I can't tell how he reacts. I'm a little nauseated, and he is so young that maybe what he means is one thing looks like another. Like me, living in this building, or me, living in Michael's townhouse. "It's cool," I say.

We both do these half waves, because it is time for Phillip to go back to his place. Maybe I should, too. I decide that I have to create a list of three other apartments I could rent before I can buy a bottle of wine. Then next, I have to see about getting a car. That would be a good idea. And I can mess it up three times before I'm out. Three strikes. This is a good plan, and I feel like it will maybe work.

My microwave beeps.

Boys Like Trees

AIDEN BAKER

The school counselor's a loser. His name is David and he's got a ponytail and thin wire glasses and he always coughs into his fist. "How are we feeling today?" he'll ask. How do we feel. As if we're in this together. He taps at his clipboard and waits for an answer. I hate the sound and I hate his question. It's how he starts every session. I don't know, dipshit. How do we? He's got this big, sad grin and I want to spit on his desk. Today, like most days, I don't. I say nothing. His philosophy, he's told me, is to let me guide our sessions. These are for you, he's said. To help you. Dumb move on his part, because when it's up to me, I choose silence.

"What are you thinking?" he prods. I choose to keep my lips slammed shut. "Nothing," I say, if anything. We spend the sessions this way, clock ticking, not talking, and then I get to go back to class.

The school pays for this shit. What a waste.

David has this painting on his wall, muted browns and tans. The painting's of a mountain and in the mountain is the face of a native man. Feathers poke out from his head and shoot into the sky. The native guy has these watery brown eyes that glare at you, real. Like he can really see you, like he's telling you something. That's how I spend most of the hour, staring at the painting, trying to read his eyes.

When Mom picks me up from school, she's either in a bad mood—
which means no talking—or she's all chipper, glimmering, non-stop
talking about the new show she's watching or new dress she's
bought or new guy she's met, talking and talking all in a rush about
whatever's got her feeling so good. Today's a good day. She's going
on and on about this guy named Steve. He's a doctor, she thinks,
which means *money,* she sings. Always, she picks the worst guys.
There was one a few months back named Harvey. He had a potbelly
and always looked at me funny. Another, Carston, smelled like
pickles. I spot the McDonald's cup in the cupholder, take it and
slurp what's left extra loud to drown her out. She looks at me from
the corner of her eye, a sad kind of look.

"How was school, Skye?" she asks, briefly opening the conver-
sational door. It's rare she invites me to speak like this. I prefer when
she doesn't.

"Fine," I say, and kick my feet up on the dashboard. I know it
pisses her off. She gives me one of her looks and goes on: Steve did
this, he's just so smart, and rich, he took me here, we ate that. I stop
listening and look out the window. Watch the trees blur.

We're in the bathroom, me and Ang, the one in the science wing
with the dated pink tile. Ang leans into the mirror, circling her eyes
with black liner. I pull out a sharpie and trace lines of grout. A maze
through the tile. No way out.

Together we huddle in a stall, pack a one hitter, blow the smoke
through a sploof. I do an impression of Ms. Astor, our geometry
teacher. We laugh so hard we choke, holding our sides.

Mom has actually made dinner: an attempt at chicken, a vegetable
medley. The chicken is tough, dry; the carrots, peas, and cauliflower have
been rendered to mush. She sits across the table from me and watches
as I push the food around on my plate. It's horrible, all of it. It feels like
a bad stage-play, and we're the god-awful actors, forced into a scene.

In the mall with Ang we walk by these boys, lanky, limbs like

Boys Like Trees

branches in oversized shirts. They grin at us with yellow teeth and I keep on walking.

"Hey, mama," one of them calls. I tug on Ang's hand and try to pull her away. But she likes the attention. She entertains them, playing bashful and dumb. They're older, taller, and I have to crane my neck to get a look at their faces. One of them has these huge nostrils like caverns, hairs poking out all aggressive. No thanks. I tell Ang we should go, but she calls me a buzzkill and lets them drag her off by the wrist. They go hook up behind the dumpsters.

I'm not upset. She's always running off like that. To be with ugly boys. She needs it, I think. Attention.

While I wait for Ang I slip into Forever 21. Lots of girls are in there, younger, in crop tops and Instagram contour. All that bronzer and highlight is too harsh for daytime. They look undead underneath the buzzing fluorescent store lights. The store's infested, full of too-young girls with debit cards. They make me sick to look at. Their exposed shoulders, sharp collar bones. I have to look away. I walk through the racks, finger the hanging clothes, the soft cotton fabric. Above me, a mannequin is perched, undressed, all curves and angles. Nausea begins to bubble up in my stomach. I head to the jewelry aisle and slip a choker into my pocket. I look around for security, for any chance I was seen. But among the hordes, I'm invisible. I sneak out with a crowd of laughing, powdered girls.

David's office smells like dust. Smells like the funeral home. Suffocating. I don't know how he stands it. Today I ask him to open the window but beyond that, I say nothing. I sit with my arms folded and look at the Native Man. I want to catch him blink.

David looks at his watch. "Time's up," he says.

Ang and I cut gym class, hide out in the cafeteria, the back tables. We split a pack of Pop-Tarts, and I break mine up into bits.

"I'd totally fuck Mr. Martinez," she says, and I gag. He's our English teacher, and he's like, a hundred years old. "Come on," she says. "You know you would, too."

I ignore that, and pull out a pair of white pills. We swallow them dry. The day becomes fuzzy, soft, like felt.

The clock hits four and then five and Mom's still not in the lot. My phone battery wanes, and then bam, a black screen. I wait, and she still doesn't come, so I walk to the 7-11. Rashid stands behind the counter, lazily flipping through a glossed magazine. On the small TV a sitcom plays. Laugh-track laughter fills the store.

"No more free donuts," he tells me, not looking up from his magazine. He used to sneak me free Krispy Kremes when I'd hang around. But I don't want a donut.

"Got any Newports?" I ask. My voice is steady. Rashid gives me a look, narrows his brows. He knows how old I am, but he sighs, slides a pack over anyway.

"For your mother, right?" he says.

I nod, and slide him a ten. He barely looks up from his magazine, but I catch a glint of it, in his eyes. The pity. It makes me feel pinned, makes me want to yell. But I don't, I head outside and sit on the curb until dusk, making my way through the pack. After a while, I stop inhaling all the way. The smoke has made my mind fuzzy, unsettled my stomach. I hold my knees and wait.

He knew us as a pair: me and my brother. We'd stop in together, grabbing armfuls of Cheetohs, Funyons, Twix. Rashid liked him, my brother; he was always slipping us free things.

When the streetlights turn on, I decide to walk home. It's six miles, but the air after dusk isn't so bad. Mosquitos nip at my ankles. I think about the girl from Mansfield Park, the one who got abducted last summer. I imagine a big white van rolling up, coming to whisk me away. Men with thick hairy arms grab me, take me, do bad things. I imagine, wait for something to happen.

There's this awful, burning smell that hits my nose as soon as I get in the house. Mom's slumped over the kitchen table, snoring. There's stew on the stove turning black. I click off the burner—there's nothing to salvage—and grab some salami from the fridge, pop a

Pepsi. I leave her there with her face smashed into the table. A Xanax zombie. Zonked.

I don't mind it, when she's like this. I get to do what I want. I could call up Ang, we could go fuck around in the forest preserve. I could steal some more pills. But I'm tired. I take my food to the den so I can use the desktop computer. The background is still set to Jason's idol, that fish-eye pic of Rodney Mullen, one leg up in the air. Seeing it always puts a rock-lump in my throat, but I can't change it. I won't.

Online, I browse through forums. Funny pictures, things that look like faces. An outlet. A car. I sip the soda in small, tiny sips, feeling the bubbles pop on my tongue.

A nudge to my shoulder wakes me. I've fallen asleep in front of the computer, again. Mom hovers above me, a mug of coffee in her hands. It's still dark out. "I'm sorry, honey," she says. "I am. I just—I want things to get back to normal."

Desperation seeps into in her voice. Her eyes look like hollow slits, her skin dry and splotchy. I decide right then: I won't forgive her.

David brought his name up once. Only once. Before that, he'd referred to him as your brother, what happened, using vague, ineffectual pronouns. He's only said his name once. It was three weeks into our sessions together.

At first, my body froze, all my muscles and bone turned completely rock-hard. Ossified, petrified, or whatever. David blinked, waited, and frozen-me looked over him, those dopey glasses and dumb ponytail and he said my brother's name plainly, flat. Like it was nothing. I froze, then woke up, raging. Don't say his name. I kicked the table, I spat. Don't you say his name. It was wrong, just wrong, hearing Jason's name come out of that loser's thin lips. He said his name like you'd say any old thing: pencil, rock. Dumb everyday things. Jason was nothing to him. I remember kicking, smashing the Connect4 board off the table, red and yellow pieces flying. I don't really remember what else, after that. Hearing his

Aiden Baker

name come from David's mouth was all wrong. It was gross. I shouldn't have to had to be there. I shouldn't have had to put up with that.

After that, he hasn't tried again. He keeps Jason's name out of his mouth. He sits back, stays quiet. I study him, his eyes, searching for that look that's become so common. I hate the look, the pity. It makes me feel not real, like I'm not me, I'm that poor girl from the paper. I hate that look so much that whenever I get it, I want to take a fork to their eyes. Thrust it in. Blind them. But as much as I hate him, David doesn't look at me like that. There's something else in his eyes. I don't know what.

The Lanky boys have started appearing in the hallway at school. They flank Ang with their gangly limbs, look at her with hungry eyes. She smiles at them, flipping her hair. I hold the straps of my backpack tight.

One of the boys licks his lips. "You wanna come over after school? Smoke some ganj?"

Hell no, I want to say, but they're not asking me. They want Ang. I look down at ugly argyle carpet, will myself to disappear.

"We'll be there," she says.

At lunch, we all sit together: Ang, me, Eliza, Marisol. Eliza picks at her salad, sips her Diet Coke. Marisol paints her nails. It's almost like before.

"I am so done with World Civ," says Ang.

"I know," says Marisol. "If we have another pop quiz, I'll kill myself."

The table gets quiet. Everyone looks at me. It happens again, I turn into a rock, just for a second. "It's fine," I say, but it isn't. It's ruined. I toss my sandwich in the trash. When I walk away, there's whispers.

David has deep purple half moons hanging under his eyes. He seems older today. I wonder if he's doing okay. He starts to say something, raps his nails on his clip-board. He starts to ask something, then stops.

Boys Like Trees

"Do you know how to play chess?" he asks.

Mom thinks I egged the Farber house. Which I did, with Ang, but there's no way she could know that. "Mrs. Farber called," she said. "What were you thinking?"

She doesn't really want to know. I keep my lips stapled shut. She grounds me, but it's whatever. I know how to get out the window. The threat means nothing to me, and it pisses her off that I'm so unaffected. She wants me to repent, to be all apologetic. *Oh Mother, I am surely so sorry!*

"Why," she asks, her voice like breaking glass. "Do you have to be so difficult?"

Her face gets red and her eyes get wet. When she gets mad, it looks like her face is a red balloon stretched too full, about to pop. She looks so dumb that I laugh. A too-loud, too-sharp laugh. She doesn't like it very much. Her face contorts and turns mean, kind of like Regan in *The Exorcist,* and I walk away.

"You ungrateful—" she shouts. My back is turned. The sentence trails off, but I can tell what she's going to say, it's still there, in the tone. You ungrateful bitch. You terrible, terrible daughter.

One time she took my bedroom door. I think she got the idea out of a movie or something, and had her boyfriend then, Tod, screw the hinges right off. I woke up to the sound of him drilling. I scrambled to cover myself with my sheets while he carried my door away.

"That's illegal," I told her. She didn't care.

To get her back, I peed into a cup and dumped it all out on the carpet. It smelled like ammonia for weeks. I played dumb, blamed Tod's dog. But Jason knew it was me.

David pulls out a big wooden board, scratched up, old, and dumps out a cloth bag full of pieces. I indulge him. This is better than Algebra, and at least I won't have to talk. The ceiling fan whirs, the only sound in the room, while he lines up his pawns in a row. I study him, his face, and try to figure out how old he is. Thirty-five, forty-five, something. I wonder if he thinks of his life as a waste. If he's given up. I slide my castle across the board. He coughs into his fist, then captures it.

When I get home, a man is at the kitchen table, slurping up Ramen. Steve, I suppose, the new guy. He doesn't look like much of a doctor.

"Hey, kiddo," he says. I groan, and walk right back out the front door.

I start with the pawns, nudging them forward. I wonder if this is a trick, if this is how he thinks he'll get me to talk. But he keeps his eyes on the board, planning his moves. He slides his pieces deliberately and rubs his palms together. I focus on the game. I can't keep track of the pieces, how they move. I invent my own rules.

Ang's mom offers to drive us, but I turn her down. I tell Ang it's so we can walk and light up a joint. Really, it's cuz Ang's mom is one of the worst offenders. She looks at me with so much pity, like she's oh so sad. I can't take it.

When we get to my house, it's empty. We put pizza rolls in the oven, we blast some Led Zeppelin. When we walk through the hall to my room, our hands full of sodas and pizza-roll plates, Ang pauses before the closed door. Posters of Rodney Mullen and Tony Hawk still taped up. A yellow "Keep Out" sign. I can tell she wants to ask, but she knows better than that.

We make it to the end of the hall and slip into my room. From an empty gallon of milk we cut a gravity bong and take turns blowing clouds out the window. The higher I get, the more I sink into my bed. Our laughter blurs and melts together. It could be like this, always. Ang. No mom. We pop pizza rolls into our mouths, we practice drawing hands. Ang lays on the other end of my bed, her bare legs glowing, smooth. A tank top strap falls off her shoulder. I can tell there's a question, still in her throat. And she asks it.

"Your mom's boyfriends," she asks, and I exhale, relieved, "you ever seen their junk?"

Boys Like Trees

I groan and throw my sketchbook at her. She laughs and laughs and laughs.

A pop quiz in Geometry. Ms. Astor's such a cow. I have no idea what the formulas are, what the angles are supposed to add to. I cheat off Jennifer Lewis, steal glances off her paper. This might as well be French. There's just no way in hell this information will ever be useful. I draw a jaguar on the last problem, a severed arm between her teeth.

Afterwards, I find Ang at her locker, leaning into one of those lanky boys.

"Do you ever get nightmares?" David asks. It's a stupid question, and I'm about to say that, but he keeps talking. "I keep having the same one, where I'm a cannibal. I know what I'm doing, and I'm disgusted by it, but I can't stop myself."

I think about it. "That's messed up," I say.

David smiles. "I know."

"Is that a real fear?" I ask. I wonder if he's one of those dudes that looks totally normal, but then has a murder dungeon in his house. If he has some weird cannibal kink. What a freak.

"Am I afraid I might accidentally consume human flesh? I don't know. I don't think so. I really don't know what it means. The mind is such a weird thing."

My mom decides we should go shopping. I don't know why, maybe they upped her meds. We go to Marshall's and walk through the aisles of clothes. She's giggling. She's got to be totally, utterly high. She picks out some horrible dresses, purple, with tulle, and forces me into them. I look like a fool, like a huge fucking loofah. She holds my shoulders, looks at us in the tri-fold mirror. "My little princess," she whispers.

I move my knight in wild L's, aiming for David's bishop. I manage to take out a pawn, but then he's got me cornered, his bishop zags, quick, and knocks out my main players. I study the board, the

Aiden Baker

squares, trying to maneuver defense, a comeback, a win. We've been playing for less than five minutes when he plucks my king. Even with my own rules, I still manage to lose.

"Again?" he asks.

We ditch gym for the fourth time this month, sit at the back tables. Ang keeps checking her phone, smiling, like she's senile. I eat my Pop-Tart in silence, watching her text. It's one of those boys, I'm sure. God, she's a lunatic, drooling.

The Lankier One is named Adam, I learn. His basement smells like mold. There's a skinny orange cat prowling around the room, a single lava lamp. Gloopy red clumps float up and down.

"Cool place," Ang lies. We sink into the musty old couch while Adam packs a bong, the glass streaked yellow-brown with resin. I doubt it's ever been cleaned. He passes to Ang, Ang to me, and I light the bowl. Inhale. It tastes like shit. Like rain water and piss. I exhale a huge cloud, and cough.

Adam fidgets with his keys. Ang giggles. I sink further into the couch, tracing the patterns on the fake wooden panels.

Geometry drags. I draw an astronaut on my graph paper, floating up and out to space. I put a crack in his helmet, imagine the oxygen leaking. Ms. Astor is lecturing in that shrill voice of hers, something about proofs. She rattles off letters: ABC, if A then D, then blah blah, yeah. Her hair is in this impossible knot on her head, a real nest. I imagine all kinds of critters lurking in there, burrowed close to her skull. She's got real horse teeth, tight lips. I wonder if she ever gets dick. I feel a buzz on my thigh, try to surreptitiously pull out my phone.

Down 2 rage 2night? Ang texts. *Big party, Forest Preserve near Elmwood.*

Always down 2 clown, I text back.

She sends a gif of Lil Yachty, fist pumping the air. I react: ha ha.

Ms. Astor clears her throat, glares her beady eyes down at me. "Can someone please remind Skye of our phone policy?"

I give her a big, fake grin and hide my phone under my thigh. But I won't apologize. I pretend to study the fat triangles she's drawn on the board. It's Friday, for god's sake. The least she could do is pretend not to see.

I take to using my queen. She can move however she likes, and I glide her regally across the board. I take out several pieces this way, but then she's captured. David moves his wrist with a flourish, and grins.

I don't know if I want to go to this party, but I know I don't want to be home. Mom is zonked again, out on the couch, so I don't even have to sneak. I empty a water bottle into the sink, drag a chair into the kitchen, stand on it so I can reach the cabinet that's over the oven. I pull out whatever's most full, brandy and gin, and fill up the bottles. It's my third time pilfering liquor, but she hasn't noticed yet. And really, she shouldn't have made it so easy.

Ang and I meet on the corner. We take big swigs from the bottles. We howl, rabid animals, free for the night. We hold hands and walk toward the train.

Adam waits for us at the station, leaning against a red brick wall. The oversized shirt should make him look small, but he looms over us, smoking a cig. I pay close attention to his face: thin lips, uneven stubble.

He grins. "You girls ready?"

"So ready," says Ang.

"I like your choker," he says, and the compliment takes me aback. I finger my neck. Ang tells me yeah, you *do* look hella good. She's got on these flowing silver shorts, blue liner rising in a triangle above her eyes. A space queen. I'm in an oversized Run-D.M.C. shirt, slick black cat-liner cutting out to my temples. It's crazy how a flick of ink can make you feel like such a bad bitch.

We hear the train before we can see it, a thunder-like rumble. It's after rush hour and we get a whole car to ourselves. The conductor gives us a look as he takes our quarters, but he leaves us

63

Aiden Baker

alone. We make fun of him as soon as he leaves the car, his big pot belly, his thick unibrow. The towns flit past, fast, and I feel big, very big. We pass the bottles between us.

He's pitched it as a party, but it's just three guys, a lame fire. Ang and I sit down on stumps. I take a big swig, maybe too big. The fire rises tall, licking up toward the sky. Almost immediately, Adam's tongue is down Ang's throat. I drink again, give a tight smile to the other three guys. They look at me with yellow eyes, wolves. I won't talk to them. They turn up the music, some trance-type shit, and I swig again, hoping Ang will get the message.

"You like to party?" One of them wants to know.

"You call this a party?" I ask. The other boys laugh. There are four of them now, maybe five, and they swirl together. One puts a hand on my thigh. They're drinking from neon Four Loko cans; they offer me one, and I take it, careful not to slur my speech, not to spill. I chug, and it's like a liquid tire. Like road-kill mixed with fake sugar fruit.

"Girl's got game," they say. I don't smile.

Soon, the trees are multiplying. The boys' eyes sharpen. They growl.

"You'll love it," he tells me. I don't know what, what I'll love. A palm extends toward me, and in it, a small paper square. I look to Ang but she's necking Adam, they look like one mega-monster straight out of Greek myth, four arms and four legs, wild snake hair. Suddenly, I don't want to be there. I take it from him.

"Just let it dissolve on your tongue."

It's not L, he tells me. Something way better. I am already fuzzed out from the alcohol, already on another plane. It takes a while to hit. And then all of a sudden, it does.

What's happening, I ask him, but words aren't with me. They come out mangled, distorted. I hear Ang laughing, or maybe she's crying, and the fire gets big, way big, around me. My legs expand, extend, I'm expansive, I'm growing into the dirt. My head balloons up and out and my skin starts to crust over, to harden. Help me, I say, or try. My words are garbled, gnarled. I'm going up, can't help it.

Breathing is hard. Labored, painful. Like swallowing gravel into my lungs. Like, I don't know. I wonder if this is a heart attack.

But no, it's not just in my chest, there's a hardening that spreads, rises all over. Vaguely, I know the boys, Ang, they've left. Vaguely, I'm aware the light changes, cracks, turns yellow again. It takes a long time before I understand: this is happening.

We ripple together, we talk through the dirt. It didn't take long to figure out how to breathe. My thoughts move slowly now, and they're all spread out, dust motes in the sun. It's quite nice here, really. Languid. Languor. Our leaves rustle and flap in the wind, the wind gentle, caring, caressing. It's easy, here, to be. Much easier, to be.

There are many of us, so so many. We communicate through dirt, signals sent through our roots. *I'm here.* I don't see him, but I feel him, there in the dirt.

The forgetting happens, naturally. Language breaks apart, decomposes. The last things I'm left with are pictures, brief flashes, an image that comes in and out. The oven door, propped open. My brother's wrist. A curved, plastic chess piece. A queen.

I spend years there, millennia. And then, as quickly as it began, I'm spat out again.

The come down takes ages. I wander out of the woods but don't want to go home. The sky is still moving like water. I walk for miles until I get to the graveyard. I fall asleep by the stones, my cheek near dew and dirt.

65

"How are we feeling?"

The ceiling fan whirs. My legs are rooted firmly on his carpet floor. David has cut his hair, cropped it short, and he yanks at his collar, coughs into his fist. How are we feeling? The same question, every damn session. Does he expect a different result? "I don't know," I say. I fidget with the hairbands taut on my wrist. I don't say it, I never say it, but of course the answer's this: like shit David. I feel like shit.

Aiden Baker

★

There's a tree we planted for him, for Jason, right by the creek near our house. It's a young tree, barely taller than me, a pale and narrow birch. I sit there some times, and I listen. It's crazy, I know, but I hear him. I know it's him cuz it's nothing corny, nothing like hey Skye, you'll be all right. *Dear Baby Sister, I Love You.* Yuck. He'd never be such a dope. His young leaves blink and shine in the wind. What he says: life is fucking funny.

Geometry

KEVIN MCLELLAN

I look out the window while sliding the clear plastic casing off from the English cucumber, cut off its ends, cut the usable bit into four cylinders and then into wedges. I remember the incident, put these curved cubes into a medium-sized stainless steel mixing bowl. Next? The Gala apple which needs dicing. I slice off two incomplete spheres, thus leaving a thick apple-wheel core. I lop off what becomes two solid ellipses. A square cylinder—the center—remains, and the remains now top the compost. Dice! Also, I dice two shallots and see that the last step involves balsamic reduction. I remember the incident yesterday. It didn't involve me, but it is so upsetting that I can no longer refer to myself in the first person.

He brings a lemon back from the fridge and then takes the glass juicer out of the two-door cupboard. Its crown-high corners, if left open, will make you bleed. He stares out the window as he juices, adds salt and pepper, mixes, and tastes. I am now on the other side of the window looking up at him. The recipe called for juice from half a lemon. I added salt and pepper, mixed, and tasted.

Artemisia

HONOR VINCENT

There is a pigeon in the studio. It is the same one that has been here each morning since your grandfather arrived in Florence, and the same one that will be here tomorrow if he leaves the windows open again tonight. He insists that night air makes paint remain pliant, but the only difference I have noticed is that my daily preparations now include picking feathers out of the linseed oil before I begin to paint.

The pigeon hides under the velvet and satin on my study table, rustling and cooing quietly. Perhaps it's nesting? It could be a nice pet for you, Zia. I'm tempted to leave it on the table and see what it does, but we've done this dance before. Yesterday I had to chase it through the easels and the cover cloths while it made its odd laughing, ooh-ooh-hooo, shitting everywhere.

Do you see its little tail poking out of the pile of cloth? I will put you down for a moment, so I can pick it up while it doesn't suspect me. Here we are! It is stronger than it looks. It would be easy for me to squeeze it hard enough to kill it. But I have a sense for you already, Zia, and I know you'll be an angry child if I make you party to such a murder. I wish that I could see it and feel it at once, this bird: I wish I could see how it twitched as I held it, I wish there was a way to record in paint such a complicated set of movements.

What do you think? Do we include this bird in the new painting? What if, instead of the head of a man, Holofernes has the head of a bird?

No, you're right, too much. We can do it in a small way. A feather escaped from the bed near the pooling blood. What about a string of dead birds drying behind Judith's maid? It will be difficult to adjust the work after I have already decided on the structure. I believe there is only room for shadow around and between the women, but there's nothing to say I can't find a place for the birds if I look. People will wonder why I put them there, and what they mean, and only you and I will know.

When I went to Cristofano Allori's studio last week, he showed me the version of Judith beheading Holofernes he is now finishing. I was darkly surprised to see how thoroughly he has flattened his Judith, and with only a few days before his customers are sending someone to pick up the painting. He's brightened her face to a whiteness so absurd it makes the composition inconsequential.

Cristo's problem is the same one he's always had. He overpaints and overworks. And he used his lover as Judith's model, losing the painting for good. In a joke with himself—perhaps this is why your grandfather insisted we meet, because I have the same inclinations—Cristo painted his face on Holofernes' severed head, and gave Judith the eyebrows of his gentle mistress. He painted only the hilt of Judith's blade, leaving out her sword entirely, in favor of focusing on her brow! Most unforgivably, there is no blood. As if you could remove a man's head without a mess.

I saw these things in the first few moments of looking at the painting because I've come to know Cristo well. I spent a long while looking and considering what I could say for the same reason. I did not ask him why he covered competent work with such a poor job of mimicry. Or what the point of painting such a story is, if he insists on painting it this way. I have learned better. I nodded, approved of his use of yellow, and returned home.

That night I worked for a very long time. I muted the yellow of my Judith's dress, deepened the shadows over her shoulders and her brow, added another spray of blood. Since that visit I have often had to stop myself from making the piece too much an argument against Cristo's. To me, to center of this painting must be the brightest part; the heart of the work remain the blade and the forearms of Judith.

Can you hear the bird shaking and shrieking in my hands now? We are just outside your grandfather's room, and still he hears nothing. He refuses to close the windows after days of my reports that they've been spitting birds into my studio; well, maybe he'll close them if it means birds in his bed when he wakes up. Let's leave the poor pigeon on his bedroom floor and close them in together. We'll see how long grandfather sleeps.

Though I complain, I am the strange one in this house for being awake so early. I assume you'll be a lady of the morning too, given your restlessness. There are servants beginning to rustle in the outer corners of the house, but our family will not come alive for several hours. They are heavy sleepers and light workers. At noon either your father or your grandfather will wander in and wonder aloud at how my painting is going, poke at their own for an hour or so, and wander away again, taking you along with them for the afternoon. While you're all gone I like to stand in the back corner of the studio and watch how the sun moves along everyone's work. You have to be able to see the image in all the many lights in which it might be seen when it's done and hanging somewhere without you.

Beyond quiet and early sunlight, I enjoy these hours because they're the only time I have to talk to you alone. I am not skilled at talking to people, and I do not believe you can hear my thoughts, so otherwise, if I don't practice now, I will be unprepared for you when you do have the sense to hear me.

It's past time to start. The pigeon left little footprints tracking red across my palette board, and splats of gray and blue on the table where it flopped through yesterday's paint. I'll have to clean up before the new model gets here in the afternoon, but first I will reacquaint myself with the work.

A painting can get away from you very quickly. If I go too long without looking at a painting of mine—and this is different for each stage of a piece, sometimes hours, sometimes days—it begins to look like the work of a stranger, and I can better appreciate its flaws and weaknesses. Each morning of working on this piece I have been relieved to find the scene is still there, and Judith, her maidservant, the blood, and the sheets are where I left them.

Blood is a tricky thing to paint. I'm not a soldier or a farmer, so I am probably getting it very wrong. I know the little streams on the bedspread look right, because those are easy enough to study: spoon wine on a cushion and watch where it goes. The spray from Holofernes's neck is more difficult. I have an appointment with the butcher where he allows me to spend a few hours watching him work each Thursday, but the blood moves so quickly, and I am often preoccupied with the crying of the animals.

No matter how close I am to finishing a work there are always adjustments to be made, so long as I'm being honest with myself. The angle of Judith's right wrist has become more unnatural over the last few days, and I finally see why. I moved the bed forward several weeks ago, and now her wrist has exaggerated a small mistake I did not think I had to fix. I will also revisit the shape of the folds in the bedsheet. The maid's face is taking on the cast of a gargoyle rather than a human being, a struggle I've been having with her from the start, for personal reasons I will tell you about when you're older.

Or perhaps now, while you can't ask me questions? I might not forgive your grandmother for dying before I was old enough to hear all of her stories. I named you for her: Prudenzia, for practicality. You will not have an awful nickname like myself or like your grandfather. Artemisia and Orazio, Arte and Ora, Art and Now, who do we think we are?

I am sorry that you will have to grow up in Florence. It's a small place, despite how its people try to make themselves feel about it. If you say this to them, they will bark its landmarks' names at you, to prove its magnificence: But the Duomo! But Santa Maria Del Fiore! Santa Croce, where Michelangelo rests? You cannot *hate* Boboli!

I give you permission, Zia, to dislike any of these places, or to enjoy them and dislike the city itself. Florence is a place without myth, without rooting, and the people who come here are quite

Honor Vincent

lost, pointing up at the monuments to say, "No no, *this* is exactly what I am!" If you are feeling especially cruel you can tell whoever congratulates you on being a Fiorentina: "Even Michelangelo Buonarroti hates this place. My mama told me so. His uncle? He wanted to be buried in Rome, as any good man would. He wanted it so badly he made sure to die there, and still the Fiorentini dragged him back up the coast, swearing 'No no, *this* is exactly where he wants to rest!' How good of a place can a city like that be?"

If you do say such a thing to anyone here I advise you to quickly walk away from whatever follows of that conversation. Whomever you were speaking to will be angry. What they have to say next will be of little value to you. It does not matter that Santa Maria is nothing but a fancily tiled copy of the Pantheon. Humor me and my other complaint about the city of Florence, as I refresh my oils and rags. The streets here bother me the most. The way the shadows fall across them, their narrowness, their lack of good, hard angles: the place looks like a painting before a painting can be made. There is nothing to do here but copy.

Your grandfather was very worried about me when we arrived, but I've calmed down. There was a time when I put my hands in the paint on my palette board, pushed and pulled until they were coated in a real mess, and I wiped them over the piece I was working on, a little practice jot of a landscape. It looked really very bad. But I was distracted and I left it in the studio to dry instead of hiding it, and I ran my hands over some of the woodwork in the hall. The next day Oro came up to my room and we had a quiet conversation about moving to the countryside. It hasn't happened

again.

I am looking forward to showing you how to paint with your own hands. I find color to be particularly delightful. I cannot wait until you see what happens the first time you wash a bit of pink over green! Looking for color in the world is like dreaming: we have the privilege of being able to stare at the shadow across the seam of a wall for hours and hours to pull out its recipe of blues and creams and oranges. And when you're mixing paints, oh! You lose your mind a bit. All of the work of painting takes a bit of mind-losing;

Artemisia

forgetting and remembering to breathe. The first few strokes after a break are the most difficult, like falling asleep with a racing mind. But once you begin, it becomes like eating, you tear and chew into the scene, you walk away with it so you can come back in the morning ready.

If I had a choice, I'd paint the streets outside my old home on Via dei Sabini forever. Rome is busy, and not with people pointing and wondering. It is many thousands of years of business and temples and popes and emperors, all of them walking over one another. It makes you choose what you are seeing at every moment. Will you watch the guards march men off to trial, or how the sun marks the wind-bitten columns of the old city, or how the children bend their arms and legs as they round the corner in a pack?

Rome is a more difficult place to live, because it also asks you to decide who you are while you look. Rebirth of Cesar, avenging and impassive? Vestal Virgin, made to stand headless in your shroud forever? Woman who rests near the catacombs on the Appia Antica, considering where to go next, or one who sits watching the street, both to soothe yourself and to see if a certain man is returning to stare at your front door? Someone who is doing God's justice, sword in hand, a force beyond yourself, or the woman who cried when she was told that a certain man was freed from prison, and because of this she will have to leave the city?

If you do return to Rome, and I hope you do, you will need to decide what you want from the city as well. Be prepared not to get it. This is why it is where people do their best work.

Look at me go on! I haven't done a thing to fix this painting yet, and I'm no longer in the mood to work on it. If I succumb and paint a street scene over it, as I *am* in the mood to do right now, my patrons would be very unhappy.

No one wants a street scene of Rome hanging in their villa, unless it's the same street scene they've seen a thousand times: Jesus being marched away as Pontius Pilate wrings his little hands. It's biblical women who are in fashion now. I've received so many commissions for Salome, Susannah, Judith, Esther. If they're dying or murdering, someone wants them, and they especially want them from me.

Honor Vincent

The way a painter's life works is that once you do a fashionable scene out of the Bible for a Medici or Colonna, they will have you do a portrait of one of their lesser family members, as a test. If you paint that third cousin well, you'll do another, and then another, until you have flattered every family member with a dream of clean hair and pearls and golden battle-armor. Those kinds of people like to have reminders that they exist above the plane of streets and bridges and river-stench, and so they put themselves floating in finery over the mantel.

You are perhaps getting the sense that your mother dislikes nearly everyone and is an unpleasant woman, but this is not true. Maria Maddalena, for instance, is a good friend of mine and the best of any Medici. I do enjoy the company of Cristo Allori, and I love your grandfather, despite how I speak of them to you. Your father is a fine enough man. I hate only one person; I know this because speaking of him gives me a headache. I suppose I'm not one for working this morning in any case, so I may as well tell you why we're doing Judith, Zia.

There was a man who was an apprentice of my father, your grandfather. His work was not promising, but he had the correct personality to convince the kinds of people he sold it to that it was. All Tassi paints is the sea and the port and frozen boats, sails as lifeless as a chipping sketch on an old serving tray.

When Tassi first saw my work in my father's studio, and me beside it, I was fourteen. He had the look of a street dog that wants something from you: cruel and hungry and stupid as a result. He asked me to marry him a few days later, and I asked him to see his work. This morning I complained to you of how flat Allori's paintings are; compared to Tassi he is a genius beyond Caravaggio. I said this to Tassi when he returned to the studio to press me, and I said other, meaner things I will not repeat here. A few weeks after his first visit my own nurse conspired to leave him alone with me. She closed her ears and eyes while he did what he did.

All I wanted during all the months of Tassi's trial was to be able to stand, alone, and bring my own charges in my own voice. During the long days of the trial, where my father and Tassi went back and forth about damages—to paintings, to my honor, to potential—I was not allowed to speak.

When I was finally called, it was after a day of confusion. They wanted to know what Tassi should be charged for, exactly. As though there was ambiguity about how we should react to what he had done.

I could not help myself but be direct. I said, "You do not care what happened to me, to my body, you didn't believe anything I say until a doctor has prodded me. I have given my testimony while you tighten the screws on my fingers like you are testing a witch—but you care that he damaged the painting that I, that my body, that these hands made? And I shook my swollen hands at them, and some of the men looked at their laps. One laughed. Most stared ahead, as though I hadn't said anything at all. They decided to put Tassi in prison for nearly a year. Pity for him. In the end, the men could all agree to one truth: Agostino Tassi stole the first Judith I made from the studio. That theft was, beyond Tassi's rape of me, or the promises he made to kill his own wife, the crime that made the Podesta angriest at sentencing.

I'll show you the scars on my thumbs from their screws when you're old enough.

If there is a lesson there, it is that things will happen to you which do not make sense, and while it will feel good to shout at the people who are doing them, there is sometimes even less sense in that.

Your grandfather pushed me to start a self-portrait after I married your father and arrived in Florence. He said it would help me move on, back to important work, and I'd be happy to have it one day. In truth he was worried about the painting I began right after the trial: an enormous mouth, opened to the edges of the canvas, dim and wet and so large it was difficult to tell what it was at al. I built up layers of heavy paint with a knife, like stucco. The canvas was inches thick. The thicker it got the more it felt like it was pulling me forward, out of my own time and into a different age. Your grandfather helped me scrape it down so I could reuse the canvas for my self-portrait.

Honor Vincent

That was nearly a year ago. I am nearly done—it's the quickest piece I've ever produced, I think. I've tried to give myself a serene expression of self-possession, but I am reading as annoyed no matter what I do. I decided also to give myself a lute, an instrument I have never played, so it is a struggle to get my hands right. I don't know why I did this. With Judith, or with Susannah, I knew where we were going. Here, with me, I don't. I recently revised the portrait to sink myself further into the shadows of the background, which makes the painting even more ridiculous: "Artemisia as a Lute Player in A Gloomy Cavern." I don't recommend this exercise to you, to take your body and put it elsewhere, to have it stare at you.

Your grandfather is awake now. Do you hear him talking to the bird? He is gentler than me. He will bring it to the courtyard and let it go, and it will return again in the morning. He will ask me about my work, and his, and my husband's, and that of the students that line the studio. We will eat dinner this evening together, and the bird will be back in the morning. And I will work on these and other paintings, until the day I can bring you back to Rome, and make it so that you can work as well.

I should be more thankful that my hands healed well and that your grandfather found a man who is content to be quiet, to marry me, and to be your father. I worry that I've forgotten grace. I will try to remember it again before you are too much older, so that my impediments don't haunt you. But for now, let's rest a while.

Artemisia

Out East on the L.I.E.

NAOMI BESS LEIMSIDER

What really happened is that Daphne shot herself in the head playing Russian Roulette on the shoulder of the L.I.E. going west toward the City—her favorite place in the whole world!—but the quack headshrinkers at school, Daphne's parents, my mother, my older sister, Carly Ann, who claimed to be Daphne's best friend, Rodney, her boyfriend, and, he insisted, her husband-to-be, rejected the real story—the truth and the heart of the matter!—as a product of my confused and disturbed mind. It was decided that I must be more than just the harmless developmentally and emotionally challenged adolescent they thought I was. I seem to be displaying psychotic tendencies: Russian Roulette is violent, inventing stories about violent behavior like Russian Roulette implies deep psychological disturbances and around and around again. They told me they are here to help me get through this difficult time so maybe I can still grow and mature into a useful adult. I told them, as always, I feel just fine.

They insisted someone evil murdered Daphne because young ladies with genius-worthy academic records, early admission to several Ivy Leagues, and the sweetest of dispositions would never resort to that kind of violence. If violent things happen, it's because violence is forced on them. This is the conventional wisdom.

When Daphne was found by the side of the great highway with a bullet lodged in her brilliant brain, they said her tragic murder was the ultimate proof of the many predators who lurk under every nook and cranny in our deranged society just waiting for a chance to strike. The world is a dangerous place for young ladies on the cusp of adulthood! What happened to Daphne was everyone's worst nightmare realized. The all-knowing authorities claimed they didn't find the murder weapon, they searched the treacherous forest on the shoulder of the lonely L.I.E. for clues, but I insisted that Daphne's father's new ergonomic Model 642 .38 special Smith and Wesson had to be there—it had to be!—and they should look dig a little deeper.

I was told, in no uncertain terms, my delusions had taken a turn for the worse. They were convinced I was trying to dirty Daphne's squeaky clean reputation. Daphne was a teen-aged girl cut down in the prime of her life on the L.I.E. and Daphne's father's gun had nothing to do with it. They told me Daphne was not, couldn't be, a willing player in her own demise. No further discussion needed. End of story.

Where is Daphne's father's gun? I asked.

They're figuring things out; they're doing the math.

Anything, anything but the truth! It certainly wasn't something they thought was ridiculous, something they considered to be out and out insane, like Russian Roulette. Certainly not.

They said: Olivia, you are in deep, deep trouble. Admit your crazy story is a lie. Repent and you will be forgiven.

If I don't, I'll deserve the punishment that will certainly come.

As far as everyone was concerned, Daphne was being appropriately treated with the proper pharmaceuticals that were the answer to smoothing the rough spots of the bumpy road that is the hallmark of being a child of divorce and a twenty-first century adolescent. Whatever that means. Modern medicine wouldn't allow violent or suicidal actions. Thank God for modern medicine! they said. After all, her prescribed pills were intelligently designed to make her as calm and content as a sleepy cat.

Out East on the L.I.E.

Daphne warned me that no one else would understand.

She said: Olivia, you're the only one.

Daphne didn't care that I'm in the Special Learners classes. She knew I am forced to take pills by the handful, that I have a mandatory twice-a-week situation with my quack school headshrinker—who are the only headshrinkers the Long Island public school system is willing to provide!—even though I was proclaimed sane and healthy last year by the young, brilliant doctor my mother and Carly Ann insisted was young and brilliant until they didn't agree with his diagnosis. Daphne didn't think I'm like my father, who is missing in action from his home in, as my mother puts it, a facility for crazies and malcontents out east. She never thought I was challenged, either developmentally or emotionally, and she believed I am smart and sane enough to bear the weight of such a complicated secret.

I asked Daphne if she was afraid she'd shoot herself, but she said she focused on the rush that came after the click, not the fear. She told me in confidence about the thrill of beating, what she called, the beast in her heart. How that victory made it all worth it.

She said: Olivia, I know I can tell you there is a beast in my heart and it will make sense to you.

I didn't know what that meant, but Daphne was the smartest girl in the Advanced Learners classes, so I knew it must mean something special.

After they found Daphne by the side of the highway, I didn't want to tell anyone anything I knew, but Carly Ann sensed a shift in me. She knew I was sitting on something important! She said, like she always does, that she needs to smooth me out, settle me down, keep me on the evenest of keels. She upped my medication, chopped some of my pills into pieces, and gave me an extra chunk along with my usual dose, which she said would calm me down enough so I could tell a clear, coherent story. Then she grabbed me by my shoulders and shook me hard.

She said: Spill it, Olivia.

★

Naomi Bess Leimsider

Carly Ann wasted no time telling Rodney because they are in cahoots. She says he is her co-conspirator. They are more than friends; they are co-conspirators. Whatever that means.

Rodney never had a problem calling me retarded, a moron, an idiot, or a time bomb. He did so frequently, despite the fact that Daphne nicely asked him not to about a million times, but Carly Ann always says she never wants to call me names like stupid or loony or psychopath even though she slips now and then. This time, she said, I've really earned all the names. When they told everyone else, Daphne's astonished parents, who actually agreed on something for the first time since their divorce, my mother, Carly Ann, Rodney, and the quack school headshrinkers, were also convinced I invented the Russian Roulette story and I was circling the drain.

I was called in for an emergency session with the quack school headshrinkers. They told me to expose the lies, to let the cat out of the bag.

Where's the cat? Where's the cat? I asked over and over much to their dismay and my amusement.

There are quack clinic headshrinkers, private practice headshrinkers, drug-pusher headshrinkers, and school headshrinkers —I've seen them all!—and then there is the young, brilliant doctor who tried to save me from all the monstrous headshrinkers with their giant horse pills served in tiny paper cups, and, occasionally, their long, thin needles filled with something, they always say, nice and smooth, something that will take me down a notch. I like to say headshrinker because it makes me think of tiny heads bobbing atop giant bodies, which makes me laugh like crazy in the headshrinkers' offices when they obviously wish I'd do something kooky like take my pants off and threaten to jump out the window so they would finally have something constructive to do like tie me up in cold sheets and jam one of their giant needles into my arm.

Both my parents were invited to speak to the quacks, but my mother told them my father can't fulfill his parental duties on account of his certifiable insanity and his current fugitive status, so Carly Ann, as usual, would replace him.

The only doctor I'm going to talk to is my young, brilliant doctor, I said. He knows everything! He understands everything! He's the only one!

My mother and Carly Ann stated that my young, brilliant doctor is a quack. A snake oil salesman in a long white coat! Not a brilliant doctor at all!

I ran around in circles trying to make heads or tails of the situation.

He's not the quack, I said. These quack school headshrinkers are the quacks! Daphne's old, not brilliant doctor is a drug-pusher headshrinker in disguise—a wolf in sheep's clothing!—and it's his fault she wanted to play a game like Russian Roulette because he pumped her full of pills and didn't understand what she meant when she said she had a beast in her heart. Don't they go to school to learn these things?

I was told to shut my stupid lying crazy mouth.

When Daphne asked to see me on the shoulder of the L.I.E. going westward toward the City, she told me she was playing Russian Roulette in her bedroom late at night with her father's brand new snag-free double action ergonomic Model 642 .38 special Smith and Wesson—he called it his stainless steel snubbed nose beauty!— that he bought when Daphne's mother demanded a divorce. Daphne's mother said that being married to Daphne's father and raising a teenaged daughter in suburban Long Island was crushing her soul. Then her mother moved out of their house and took a one-way trip on the L.I.E. to an apartment in the City where she could, she said, start again from scratch. Her father went gun shopping and started a profile on several matchmaker websites. Daphne didn't want her father hanging out in those dark, seedy corners of the internet, but he told her if he wanted her opinion about his sex life he would ask, and, besides, wasn't it worse that her mother had run off like the slut she is so she could hook up with strange men in the City? Then Daphne's mother said her father was using her epiphany that their married life was a sham by trying to create an old man's version of his youth in a desperate attempt to recapture lost glory. She told Daphne that her father is a pig and a liar and he cheated on her a thousand times, but Daphne, who got along really well with her father before her mother left, told me he cries at night when he thinks she's sleeping.

Her mother called her father a lunatic for many reasons, even though, as far as I knew, he wasn't like my father at all, and she said that keeping a loaded gun in the same house where his teenaged daughter lives is absolutely the sign of a man who has completely lost his mind. He was obviously not interested in protecting his brilliant beautiful daughter from all the crazy people who come through windows and steal pretty girls and be all too happy to find a gun in the house, but Daphne's father said if she was so concerned about his paternal qualifications, she should have thought of that before moving to the City and pretending she didn't have a family. He insisted his Smith and Wesson, his snubbed nose beauty, wasn't just a weapon; it was dependable, reliable. Unlike someone he knew.

Daphne thought this turn of events was humiliating and disturbing. The adult world seemed so hopeless and chaotic.

Macabre, she said.

Daphne waited until her father went out on dates with the women he met on the message boards, then she snuck into his room, borrowed the loaded Smith and Wesson lying loose in his bureau underneath his cholesterol medicine, bargain-store condoms, and porno magazines, and made her way through the thicket that separated suburban Long Island from the dark shoulder of the L.I.E.

She said: Olivia, the beast has swallowed me whole.

I tried to comfort her. I reminded her that her father could be like mine—an out and out lunatic, as my mother and Carly Ann like to call him—but it didn't seem to work. I thought my young, brilliant doctor could rescue Daphne from this beast—after all, he is young and brilliant!—since her old and far less brilliant doctor obviously wasn't doing a very good job of it. Daphne appreciated my offer, but told me it was too late for all that. She found the answer all on her own.

★

The night after Daphne's funeral, her parents invited Rodney, Carly Ann, all of the students from the Advanced Learners classes. Carly Ann told me Daphne's parents didn't want me there because I'm the dangerous psycho girl of Long Island who tells evil tales, but after begging her to try and change Daphne's parents' minds she said she would. Her parents relented and said I could come if I apologized for insisting to anyone who would listen that their obviously murdered daughter killed herself playing Russian Roulette with her father's gun.

If I repented, I would be forgiven.

Daphne's parents put up dozens of pictures on a huge posterboard of Daphne as a little girl with sugar cone clown sundae all over her face and clothes. They didn't ask what we wanted, they just ordered something like a hundred sugar cone clown sundaes, left them all on the table they reserved for us, and argued about the bill for the ice cream and for the funeral.

I ate the sugar cone clown sundae faces, the cherry licorice clown hair, the sour gumdrop noses, the jellybean eyes, and the sprinkles outlining the chubby cheeks. The faceless sundaes melted.

It was a macabre party.

The sadness made me quiet and Rodney kicked me in the shins under the table to get a rise out of me, just to get me started. I kicked him back for making me want to act out on a night like this. I didn't care that Rodney had just lost the only girlfriend he ever had to Daphne's father's snubbed nose gun.

This is Daphne's day, so don't start, I said.

You're just like your father, Olivia, Rodney said.

I tried to smack him across his ugly, stupid face.

Olivia! Carly Ann said. That's enough.

Daphne didn't want to marry him, I said.

Rodney regarded me with his squinty, birdy eyes.

Knock it off, Olivia, or I'm taking you home, Carly Ann said.

I took a giant bite from my third sugar cone clown sundae and opened my mouth to show Rodney. Carly Ann threw my sundae in the garbage and pushed a handful of pills in my face.

Naomi Bess Leimsider

I don't have any water, I said.

I don't care, Carly Ann said.

I swallowed them dry. They only stuck a little in my throat, but I threw myself on the floor anyway and pretended I was choking.

Stop it, Carly Ann said. Control yourself.

The clowns are blind, I said. I ate their eyes.

Olivia, Carly Ann said.

I heard the warning, but I leaned in and whispered the truth in her ear anyway.

Daphne wanted the future to be a surprise, I said. What would happen next? Would she be alive to see the next moment and the next moment or would she destroy her own soul? Pulverize it, liquify it until the glob of matter known to the small, suffocating world of Long Island as Daphne no longer existed in the universe! When she put the gun to her head, for just a few moments she was happy and at peace. She wanted to shoot the beast out of her head.

Carly Ann shuddered a bit as if she saw a ghost. I looked around for Daphne's fluttering soul, but it was nowhere to be found.

I started my fourth sugar cone clown sundae.

Carly Ann, my mother, and all the quacks tell me at the rate I'm going I will definitely end up like my father who had to be hospitalized a hundred times last year before my mother decided to commit him for the rest of his life or whenever he regains his sanity, whichever comes first. When my father started refusing to take his pills, my mother set up a cot for him in the basement. She told me to stay away because his crazy was obviously catching. Every once in a while, my mother unlocked the basement door to check on him, to make sure he was taking his pills and not swinging from the rafters like a monkey.

He's free to roam around the room, my mother said. If it were up to me, he'd be hanging in chains.

My father pretended to swallow his pills, but he just spit them out and let them melt in his warm palm. He said they made him thirsty and white bubbly goo formed in the corners of his mouth. His spotty tongue darted in and out like a crazy lizard. He drank can after can of lemon soda because he said he needed a crisp refreshing drink he could rely on and that is the flavor the television told him to buy. He told me that without the pills he can feel his organs pulsing and humming in his body. When he's taking them—and my mother says he's a crazed animal without them—he claims the earth is a dull, flat place. Gray and shadowy. A hell of sorts.

Shh, he'd whisper, and put one of his fingers to his dry, pasty lips. Not a word to anyone, Olivia.

A few months later, an ambulance came in the middle of the night with armed police officers riding shotgun. They took him away on a stretcher with a mask clamped over his face shushing him over and over on the way out the door. He yelled, Olivia, don't let them take the beautiful world away from me! My little girl knows! Ask her! Ask her!

My mother said: Oh for Christ's sake, make him take his pills, will you? He's a crazed animal without them.

I protested by holding my breath until I knew my face was a deep scary blue and my heart was ready to pop.

My father is now on the run. A fugitive.

On the lam, my mother said.

I pictured him stooped over, exhausted, sitting on a lamb, and hoping the small, fuzzy animal will take him far, far away.

My mother said that if I keep on going the way I'm going, someday soon something similar will happen to me.

My mother and Carly Ann have taken me to hundreds of thousands of headshrinkers. I am seriously hyperactive, deeply disturbed, mentally borderline, intellectually deficient. I have been taking pills since the beginning of time.

After my father was sent east on the L.I.E. toward the Sound, I threatened to slice up my legs with my mother's pink razors, cover the bloody spots with tiny puffs of cotton, and go to school so I could scare the quack headshrinkers. When my mother instructed Carly Ann to find me a new doctor, one who would do the necessary tests and find the right pharmaceutical combo to halt my similar slide into complete crazy, Carly Ann found my young, brilliant doctor.

My young, brilliant doctor was the youngest Harvard Med graduate ever. A certifiable genius! I asked Carly Ann if he was smart like Advanced Learners smart and she said smarter. She said he was going to fix me.

My young, brilliant doctor was tall and gorgeous. Freshly scrubbed and glowing.

I smiled at him. Big. My lips turned up at both corners like a clown.

My gigantic file lay open on his tidy desk. Everything in order. Everything in place. He knew everything!

He glanced at my mother.

So you think it's Graves' disease? he said. Or she's bipolar? Maybe paranoid schizophrenia?

Which one is it, my mother asked. Carly Ann has read online that the kind of behavior Olivia displays can be the manifestation of a physical disorder or the beginning of a slow slipping into madness. So far, nobody knows. We are counting on you.

Why don't we see what's going on, he said.

My young, brilliant doctor pushed his yummy hands into my throat, studied my face and neck for a long time with a tiny light that gave me a headache, and I stared deep into his wondrous blue eyes like the middle of the ocean or a perfect summer sky.

Who's Grave? I asked. Does he know I have his disease?

Olivia has a long history of inappropriate behavior, my mother said. She's also a liar, just like her father.

Do you tell tall tales, my young, brilliant doctor asked me.

Only when the short ones aren't true, I said.

Do you believe things that aren't real or see things that aren't there? he asked.

How would I know, I giggled.

He winked at me.

I think she's fine, he told my mother.

I grinned at my young, brilliant doctor.

She needs to be examined, my mother said. You think you're

the first doctor we've seen? Olivia has her father's genes, doesn't she? She's going to end up like her father, isn't she?

I don't know what's going on with her father, but Olivia's not showing any signs of a noted disorder, mental or otherwise, my young, brilliant doctor said. In my medical opinion, there's nothing wrong with her.

He tapped me lightly on the back.

In fact, she seems pretty hardy, he said.

His hands were so gentle and yet so strong! They were tender meaty forces of strength.

She needs something that will fix her, my mother said. Carly Ann told me she read about millions of possibilities. Do some tests.

My young, brilliant doctor wavered for a moment.

Now, my mother said.

He made a few notes in my file and then busied himself at his tidy doctor's desk with his carefully arranged doctor things before coming back with several vials and a long needle.

I'm fine, I said. Promise.

Not another word, Olivia, my mother said.

I smiled at my young, brilliant doctor.

He smiled back!

He wrapped the rubber tube tight around my upper arm and swabbed it in one neat maneuver. He pushed the needle in so slowly I didn't feel the bite of the tip. He is an expert in all things. I watched my blood pour into tiny plastic containers.

We need the results as fast as possible, my mother said.

I winked at my young, brilliant doctor.

He winked back!

I'll call you, he said. But he looked at me and not at my mother.

We connected for a moment—like we had kissed!—our souls intertwined, and I saw his kind, genius soul.

My young, brilliant doctor and I were in love!

I grabbed one of his hands. It was so big and soft! He clasped his fingers into mine for a split second—I swear he did!—but then his fingers wiggled and pushed against mine. I let go of his young, brilliant hand.

Naomi Bess Leimsider

My young, brilliant doctor straightened his doctor coat and fiddled with his Harvard Med pen.

On the way home, I sat backward in the station wagon trunk. I stuck my head out the window and gasped at the rush of wind in my face. It was fresh and good and when I opened my mouth it was like drowning.

Carly Ann, what should we do, my mother said.

Let's bring her up to two hundred milligrams, Carly Ann said. Then we'll do a watch and wait.

I thought he was supposed to be so brilliant, but it seems that your sister is the real genius around here, my mother said loud enough so I didn't miss a word.

Carly Ann turned around to get a good look at me, but when our eyes met she refused to let me in.

I wish I knew Carly Ann when she was first born. They bonded, those two, before I could defend my right to exist. Right from the moment Carly Ann was born, my mother saw something in her; a kindred spirit, an ally. I have no memory of Carly Ann until she was already powerful and strong. A force I couldn't reckon with.

Two hundred milligrams enveloped me in a thick, buttery fog that warmed me like my young, brilliant doctor's sweet pie hands.

You must be driving Daphne insane, Carly Ann told me a few weeks before Daphne murdered the beast that invaded her brain. Rodney says she's getting to be a pain in the ass, and, frankly, he blames you.

Why, I asked.

She told me she wasn't well, Carly Ann said. I asked her what was wrong—what could possibly be wrong with her perfect life?—and she said sometimes she just falls down the rabbit hole, as if that's supposed to make sense. I told her it was just because she and Rodney were fighting, but after I told Rodney what Daphne told me—because he had to know—he told her mother so she could get a few sessions with one of the school docs. Rodney told me the sessions worked, she started taking her pills, and Daphne went back to her perfect life. Then she started hanging out with you, Olivia. Daphne thinks she has the most problems, the most to deal with all the time, but she just wants attention. And let me tell you, Olivia, you certainly give her that. You're always mooning over her.

I'm not mooning, I said. She's my friend, too.

She's not your friend, Carly Ann said.

She is too, I said. She tells me important things.

Like what, Carly Ann asked.

Nothing, I said.

She's telling you how much she hates me, Carly Ann said.

Why would Daphne hate you?

She must have told you Rodney bought her an engagement ring, Carly Ann said.

She didn't, I said.

Well, he did, Carly Ann said. Rodney wants her to be his wife. He even asked Daphne's parents permission for her hand in marriage. That's the kind of guy Rodney is. She didn't tell you that, did she?

Does she want to marry him?

Don't be ridiculous, Carly Ann said.

Daphne doesn't love him, I said.

Olivia, you don't know what you're talking about, Carly Ann said. This all goes way over your head. You've never even kissed a boy.

When will I kiss a boy, I asked.

Probably never, but who knows, Carly Ann said. Stranger things have happened.

89

I imagined my young, brilliant doctor's lips touching mine. A man's mouth. Not like one of the stupid boys in the Special Learners class who can't even understand our assigned short versions of important books—the slim ones with poorly drawn pictures—that Rodney always makes fun of to my face. Those are the boys I have to choose from. The smart boys in the Advanced Learners classes who will grow up to be brilliant men just like my young, brilliant doctor are as far out of my reach as the moon.

Naomi Bess Leimsider

My young, brilliant doctor promised he'd call. I believed that someday I'd pick up the phone and hear his voice.

Daphne asked to meet me after school at the edge of the great highway, the L.I.E. going west toward the City, where the dense forest meets the shoulder.

Let's run across, Daphne said.

The cars are going too fast, I said. We'll get hit.

If we're smart about it, we'll just take a deep breath and fly across, Daphne said.

I don't understand, I said.

Daphne took my hand and we flew across—we barely touched the ground!—with a power like an earthquake or a hurricane. An organic force that couldn't be stopped. In less than a second, we were on the gray cement partition.

See? Daphne said.

She wasn't even out of breath.

The cars rushed past us so fast my stomach dropped and I had to suck air back into my lungs. The rest of the world receded. The shoulder was a million miles away.

How will we get back, I asked.

Daphne took out a full bottle of her pills and spilled them on the ground.

I'm not going to take these anymore, Daphne said.

Won't they know if you don't take them, I asked.

How will they know? Daphne asked.

They can test your blood, I said. Or pump your stomach.

Nobody's pumping my stomach, Olivia, Daphne said.

That's what my mother told me, I said. She makes me take them in front of her and she opens my mouth to make sure I've swallowed them. Once I ate a mouthful of mints so she wouldn't be able to tell, but that didn't work because she said she'd get my blood tested and my stomach pumped so she'd know for sure.

Your mother's crazy, Daphne said.

I buried the pills with dirt. I made little dirt coffins for Daphne's dead pills.

Rodney says I make life more difficult than it has to be, Daphne said. He says he'll make everything simple for me.

I know, I said.

Carly Ann told you?

I nodded.

We've been going out since junior high, Daphne said.

Do you want to marry him?

Love does not bloom in the eighth grade, she said.

Daphne picked her pills out of their coffins so they could rise from the dead.

I'm going to tell you something important, she said. Nobody else will understand but you.

I can keep a secret, I said. I'm not stupid.

I know you're not, Olivia, but sometimes even smart people can't keep secrets, Daphne said.

You can trust me, I said.

I've been playing Russian Roulette, she said.

What's that?

A game of chance, she said.

What are you chancing? I asked.

I put my father's loaded gun to my forehead, then it's wait and see, Daphne said. The moment before I pulled the trigger the first time was the most amazing moment of my life. Remember I told you about the beast? For a few seconds, the beast was quiet. I know when I tell you there is a beast living in my head it makes sense to you.

I nodded.

The first time I did it, a split second before I pulled the trigger, I peed myself, Daphne said. Soaked right through my pajamas and onto my bedspread. I thought my heart was going to explode! Then I pulled the trigger. And nothing. Just a click. I put the gun back in the drawer, went back to my room. My father thought the Smith and Wesson was just his consolation prize, but it is so much more! Everything was suddenly clear. I understood the past and I could see into the future! I became a prophet! A soothsayer! After that, I fell asleep, and I was really out cold, because when my dad came in

91

Naomi Bees Leinsider

to say good night he found me in my own pee. I told him I was sick. I changed my pajamas and drank the tea he made for me. He didn't say anything, but he left my pills and a glass of water by my bed. I even ran a fever for the next few days. I was converted, Olivia! It was my conversion sickness! I figured out a way to quiet the beast all by myself. I kept going back to the moment right before the click, when I was limited just like everyone else. When I didn't want to know what would happen next. Were there ramifications for my actions? Would I be alive to see the next moment and the next moment? Would the beast destroy my soul? Pulverize it, liquify it until the glob of matter known to the small, suffocating world of Long Island as Daphne no longer existed in the universe? Or would I kill the beast? As soon as I heard the click, I knew I was on to something special. When I heard that click, I tasted the danger, and I pulled back from the abyss. I kept the beast at bay! I understood everything! I was truly alive!

But what if you shoot yourself in the head? I asked. How do you know you won't shoot yourself in the head?

Daphne threw her pills, one by one, into the confusion of the L.I.E. They were crushed by thousands of thunderous wheels.

I'm just trying to quiet the beast, she said.

She threw the amber bottle in after the pills.

If I do, she said. I'll be a willing player in my own demise. Do you understand?

Yes, I said. I do.

Daphne moved a few steps toward the edge of the gray cement slab that separates the L.I.E going west toward the City and east toward the Sound. She opened her mouth, took a deep, jagged breath, and leaned into the traffic.

I could be her savior!

I grabbed her, wrapped my arms around her stomach, pushed in both my arms as if she was choking, and pulled her back to the safe middle.

Daphne turned to face me.

I knew I could trust you, she said.

Out East on the L.I.E

Her eyes bore into mine.

Now it's your turn, she said.

I shook my head.

Do you trust me, she asked.

Yes, I said.

Okay, then, we'll take it one step at a time, she said. Hold your breath.

I gulped some air and held it still in my lungs.

Walk to the edge, she said.

I took a baby step or two toward oblivion.

Plant your feet, lean in a little, and just sway in the wind, she said. Exhale slowly. You won't fall. I've got you.

I couldn't do it. The air escaped from my lungs in a whoosh and the force of the L.I.E. pushed me back. The highway rumbled under my feet like an awakening monster. It wanted to open its giant yawning mouth and swallow me whole.

Daphne turned away from me and stood in the middle of the great highway facing east. Her arms spread wide like an eagle; her eyes turned up to the sky.

After a while, the zooming cars slowed to a stop and they inched along every couple of minutes.

My father used to say he wasted half his life sitting in the goddamned parking lot on the goddamned L.I.E., I said. He always said the thought of so much of his life wasted made him want to run screaming.

The people peeked through their car windows and stared at us like we were aliens. Daphne refused to acknowledge the busy world around her. She sat Indian-style with her back perfectly straight and her eyes closed.

Carly Ann said you're in love with Rodney, I said.

She was quiet for a long, long time.

Carly Ann and Rodney are in cahoots, she finally said.

What does that mean, I asked.

After a while, she opened her heavy eyes and gazed at me.

I'm in love with my young, brilliant doctor, I said. Is that crazy?

She smiled.

Naomi Bess Leimsider

It's not not crazy, she said and closed her eyes again.

I curled up like a cat at her feet.

The morning Daphne was discovered with a bullet lodged in the beast in her brain, Carly Ann greeted me with a dose of my pills and a tall glass of water. Her eyes swollen and slitted. Her face puffy and pale like a potato.

Swallow, she said.

I pretended to swallow my pills.

Drink, she said.

I gulped the water.

Open your mouth, she said.

I opened my mouth and she rooted around like I was a squirrel hiding acorns for the winter.

Swallow them, she said.

I made swallowing motions.

Olivia, she said. I have to tell you what happened to Daphne. It's difficult enough for the rest of us, so it's something you really might not understand.

I went to see my young, brilliant doctor. I called his office and tried to make an appointment, but his nurse said he didn't have an opening for months. I told her I've been waiting forever and ever for him to call.

The doctor is booked solid right now, she said.

When I showed up at the door, the nurse reminded me that my young, brilliant doctor is a busy man.

I'll wait, I said.

94

If only he'd be curious enough to peek into the waiting room and look for his rogue patient! It might take him a moment, but then he'd recognize me. Our eyes would meet, and I'd connect again with the windows to his kind, genius soul.

I'd kiss him with a force as strong as the zillions of cars on the L.I.E.! I'd throw my arms around him and hold on tight like one of the cold wet sheet packs they wrap my father in when he's off his pills and acting, my mother says, bat shit crazy. Then my young, brilliant doctor would understand the depth of our connection—our intertwined souls!—and he'd kiss me back.

My first real kiss!

His lips would be sweet and delicious like orange slices, and I'd suck out the pulpy sweetness until all he had left was the briny shell. His lips would be rich and smooth, like a thousand ice cream sundaes with tons and tons of creamy whipped cream and millions of juicy cherries on top. I'd spoon up giant mouthfuls.

After a long time, the nurse said my young, brilliant doctor would see me. She directed me through the tangle of exam rooms to his office.

Everything was different! Everything had fallen apart! His doctor things were so neat and orderly when he pulled so much blood out of my body. He was so perfect in his pinch, so effortless in his draw! Books were now pulled off the shelves, their spines broken. Patient files scattered, cold coffee in chewed styrofoam cups, and half-eaten pastries stuck to the surface. Mugs full of old cigarette butts. His needles and rubber tubes in clumps.

Olivia, he said. How can I help you?

My heart thumped so hard I thought my chest would burst open.

You were supposed to call, I said.

What do you mean, he said.

You said you were going to call, I said. You didn't.

My young, brilliant doctor flipped through my enormous file.

I don't call, he said. One of the nurses does. Your mother was contacted a few months ago.

I sat down hard in his giant patient's chair. I sank into the slippery velvet cushions.

My young, brilliant doctor's face had yellowed. There were new dark circles, tender and bruised like chicken skin, under his eyes. His face was softer and rounder, loose folds under his strong, brilliant chin and new creases around his eyes. Deeper lines around his mouth. His stomach was a slab of flesh over his pants. He kept his

Naomi Bass Leimsider

doctor coat buttoned over his middle. He checked his watch, then the clock on the wall.

He closed my file, offered me a handshake, and waved one arm toward the door.

My young, brilliant doctor was not brilliant. He would not have been able to help Daphne. He wouldn't have known what to do. Like all the other thousands and thousands of doctors, he would have made promises he couldn't keep. Lied to her. Told her he was a genius—with a kind, caring soul!—who was capable of dragging the beast out of her head with his bare hands and stitching her back up good as new. Told her she'd be free forever from all beasts so she could go on to medical school and live her life on her own, without Rodney, like the Advanced Learner she is.

The truth is that my young, brilliant doctor would have broken her heart.

Daphne's dead, I said. They found her on the shoulder with a hole in her head and they're all out on the L.I.E searching for the evil person who killed her. Where is her father's gun? The truth is staring them in the face, but it doesn't matter. They're too busy tacking up pictures of Daphne with ice cream all over her face up and down the highway. It was the beast! It was too strong for her. Her quack headshrinker is old and not brilliant! He gave her more pills, they made her take more and more and more and more pills, but they couldn't kill the beast.

My young, brilliant doctor didn't say a word. Didn't look at me. Stayed fixated on my huge, messy file. His hand twitched in the direction of his phone.

I stared deep into what used to be his wondrous blue eyes. My heart ached for him, for the young, brilliant doctor I once knew.

I moved toward him like an organic force that couldn't be stopped! I shouldered my way like a cat on the hunt! I pulled his face down to my level with both my hands and kissed him hard. With the force of a zillion cars on the L.I.E.! Smashed my lips against the teeth in his opened, shocked mouth.

I ran out of his office—I barely touched the ground!—but the people in the waiting room didn't notice anything was different or wrong. They sat obediently in their bolted chairs, with their legs crossed and their magazines opened in their laps, waiting their turn to be touched by what they thought was his youth and brilliance, so they could be healed forever and ever.

After I returned home, I made the inevitable descent to my father's basement room. I found my father there, sitting on his cot stuffing a dilapidated suitcase, with torn, brown newspapers, old t-shirts, dirty socks, and empty cans of lemon soda like he had never left. His thin, pale skin was greenish, khaki, like army fatigues or pea soup. He was dressed in his clay-colored jumpsuit, his uniform, from the loony bin. He looked like a hallucination; a wavy hologram figure; a shimmering ghost. Ashy and unearthly. The living dead.

Hi, Daddy, I said.

I'm starving, my father said. Do you have any chocolate?

Are you feeling all right, daddy? I asked.

I'm fine, my father said. Promise.

Where have you been?

Out and about, he said.

Where are you going, Daddy?

Can you keep a secret?

Yes, I said.

My father shoved one more newspaper into the suitcase and locked it. He walked toward the door, then turned around and looked me deep in my eyes. He searched for my soul.

All roads lead east toward the Sound, he said.

I don't understand, I said.

He brought one finger to his dry lips, and then he was gone.

My mother and Carly Ann said we were going for a ride in the car, said we were going to Daphne's favorite ice cream shop for sugar cone clown sundaes. They attempted to tease me out of my hiding place with promises of treats, but I hid in my father's now forever empty basement room because I knew.

Ice cream sundaes, Olivia! they said.

Naomi Bess Leimsider

The quack school headshrinkers said I left my mother and Carly Ann with no choice. They said they tried everything. They didn't know if I was capable of understanding, but I told them that was ridiculous. I learn things all the time!

Olivia! they said. Ice-cream!

In an upside down world, Daphne and I would meet again on the L.I.E. We'd be in the middle of the fastest place on Earth standing perfectly still on the slim strip of cement that kept us safe. The truth is elusive and malleable, I'd tell her, and she'd nod because she finally understood.

If it were up to me, I would have lived the rest of my life under my father's old cot, but my mother pulled me out by my feet and dragged me to the door.

Carly Ann sat in the front seat of the car.

I know we're not going to the ice cream shop, I said.

Carly Ann turned around to look at me.

I met her gaze. We didn't move.

The air was still: the calm before the storm.

My mother got into the car and slammed the door so hard behind her the whole world felt like it could break open. Carly Ann broke our connection and turned to face the great highway that lay in front of us.

We headed east on the L.I.E. toward the Sound.

Lady: Part I

SWATHI DESAI

The Man has come to visit almost every day of Kavita's summer vacation. He says he comes to visit her uncle, Dilip *Masa*, but he spends most of his time with Amita *Masi*, the pretty aunt. The Man makes Kavita laugh, he tickles her, he says funny things, makes her feel special, says she looks like a lady in her finery. "Everyone will be watching you at my sister's wedding, she will be so jealous of you," he teases.

Her uncle teases her, too, but he never looks at her like The Man does, like the boys back home who stare at girls on Main Street at night without smiling or even saying anything. Sometimes they call out strange names to the girls as they pass. She doesn't understand what the words mean, but the girls giggle when they hear them or sometimes yell bad words back at the boys hanging out the car windows. The Man is younger than her father or he would be married and have kids now. And he must be older than Dilip *Masa*, because her uncle is still in school. The Man seems to exist somewhere in between college and marriage.

Kavita wears her new clothes to the wedding, running her hand over the saffron colored silk, fingering the little mirrors encased in red thread like a frame. Kavita hears The Man shout, "Lady," when he sees her in her new party clothes. She doesn't feel like a lady, she is still a girl, almost ten. When she doesn't turn to look at him, he whistles long and slow, like she has heard the boys do to the high school girls back in California. She pulls her shawl around her shoulders and bends her face down, managing a smile, she doesn't want to seem rude. "Lady," he shouts again, louder. "You look like such a pretty lady." He laughs and nudges his three friends, who all look like him: slicked back hair, big black mustaches, wearing silk *kurtas* over matching pants that look like baggy pajamas.

The wedding is loud, chaotic, thrilling. Under the wedding canopy, the pundit spouts words in a language she doesn't understand, throwing colored powder at the fire. Kavita thinks she can see every single star in the night sky. She has been given special permission to stay up late because the astrologer has deemed the most auspicious time for the wedding to be just before midnight. There will be fireworks, too, her *Masis* have promised. Her most favorite holiday is the 4th of July. Suddenly she misses California, her friends, her bed. After a long time of waiting, her aunt, the nice *Masi,* tells her the ceremony is almost over. The beautiful bride walks slowly, keeping her head bowed as she follows her betrothed around the fire, carefully walking the seven steps, mirroring the seven vows.

"Why does she look so sad?" Kavita asks.

"Because she knows, soon she will have to leave her parents for her mother-in-law's house, never to return."

"Never?"

"Well, not never, it's symbolic."

"Brides are just sad, I guess," she says. Her aunts giggle.

Sleepy and bored, Kavita wanders past the wedding canopy, near a group of men who all look like The Man with their big mustaches and slicked back hair. They look drunk because they are teetering about, tripping and laughing hard. It reminds her of a New Year's Eve party at her house; one of the uncles was dancing strangely and her father tried to get him to sit down. "Drunk!" The uncle's wife shouted after he threw up on the floor. If she can find someone familiar, they might be able to tell her when the fireworks will begin. Turning to go back to the canopy, she sees The Man. He will know where to find the fireworks.

Lady: Part I

Kavita is flying, hovering above the wedding canopy, a specter floating in the wrought iron sky, humming the song the women below her have gathered to sing. The tune can't drown out the sound of The Man panting in front of a young girl's frozen form, his breath ripe with the odor of *bhang* and liquor. Though she can still hear the women singing, she can't comprehend all the words. But she understands the nature of the song; a bride must let go of her parents to be with her beloved for the rest of her life. The song's lyrics are not enough to make her shed tears, it is the melody, the atonal pitch that calls to her and binds her spirit in its melancholy. The Man's cries penetrate the tapestry of the women's folk song. She floats above the scattered groups of the wedding guests, searching for someone, anyone who can save the girl. All the familiar warm faces are hidden from her as she drifts further away from the girl below, powerless to stop the anguish.

She wakes up alone, all the beds on the terrace empty, unmade. The sun burns her face and arms, the only extremities outside the bedsheets. The heat, heavy on her eyes, becomes almost intolerable, prodding her awake. Under the sheets, the cold, damp urine clings to her underwear, the sheets, soaking all the way through to the mattress. She is too old to be wetting the bed. Maybe her mother won't be angry with her. She feels eyes looking at her, spying upon her. The three mammoth vultures balance on the terrace ledge, their shiny black feathers slick and formidable, their red gristly necks and beaks terrify her and keep her cornered on her bed, paralyzed. She hears quick footsteps on the terrace; her mother shouts, screams for the predators to get away. She hits the beasts with a broom, the thick straw makes a dull thudding sound as she beats them. They do not think anything of her assault and the violence does nothing to shift their focus. Unfazed and unimpressed with her theatrics, they coolly await their prey.

Audree Begins to Speak

TAMARA JAFFE

I. Earth

His face changed when I told him that I'd started exercising again. We were eating dinner together at the time, baked salmon with dill, rice, green beans—something I made easily—he started eating with one face and ended with another. Everything about the face moved at once, as if a lever had been switched, and a new face covered the old. The muscles moved a millimeter to the left, the eyes narrowed, and something that ordinarily supported the structure of the face deflated. It's possible that my training causes me to pay too much attention to physiognomy. He said, "I thought you'd stopped exercising!"

But that man's crises mean nothing to me anymore. I have enough aggravation without him. Just yesterday, when my boss asked, "Can I get a hug?" it wasn't a question. We were in the black-topped parking lot outside the Foot Psychophysiology Building, the largest parking lot at the university, and I was very near my car, but not close enough. I couldn't turn toward it and pretend I didn't see him. He's young and tall, with shiny black hair and a black goatee with the hair growing up around the sides of his mouth into a mustache. He has a model's high cheekbones. He wears citrus-musk cologne. I am a photographer, and my eyes know that his body is photogenic, but his demand for the hug made me feel like I was hugging a sack of nice-smelling sand shaped like a tall man. I wouldn't have minded hugging sand. I wanted to go home. My stomach leaned away from the embrace, but the rest of me knew I couldn't. I looked at the sun in the blue afternoon sky and remembered that I was not alone. Many women have been here. Maybe even in this parking lot with this man.

What I do for a living is an important part of this story. I work on people's feet. When their toes are crooked, not bending right, they have pain in their arches, they can't bend their foot, or they have trouble standing, they come to me and I take pictures. You would think that looking at their feet in person might be the way to know and see what the trouble is, but it's the pictures that tell the truth. Pictures show the exact condition of feet. I analyze the line along the top of the foot that slopes down from the ankle, and I examine the tendons that pop up like puppet strings connecting the toes to the ankle. It is also part of my job to know that in some countries there is jewelry for the foot that approximates those tendons, and to know the history of that jewelry.

I also study the patterns in a footprint. Did you know that footprints are similar to fingerprints? None are alike. Foot reading is less popular in the West than palmistry, although the swirls on the foot can be interpreted as easily as those on the palm. People who do such readings usually misinterpret what they see because of their own and their client's magical thinking. But what exists in our bodies is real, and we can understand it. What exists is real. Beliefs exist. Beliefs are real. I think that's a syllogism, but I don't remember. Beliefs are among the most powerful and misunderstood forces in the universe. I believe that if I take clear pictures, and pay attention to my clients, they have a chance of getting an accurate diagnosis, which may help them manage their condition. I don't know if this is true, but this belief makes my work tolerable, and sometimes enjoyable.

We can understand what has happened to the body in the past, and we can participate in its development in the future, but we

103

Tamara Jaffe

cannot change the material truth of the body itself. Foot psychophysiology is science, and sciences exist because scientists demonstrate their willingness to be wrong in order to approach a more accurate understanding of the physical world. When humans refuse to know what is real, science—and humans—will vanish. What is real will remain. Footprints can be used to identify bodies that have been badly mangled in a plane wreck. The grooves, bumps, and wart outcroppings are unique, and are often preserved in a crash, due to the shoe's protective function, even when the rest of the body is decimated.

I take hundreds, sometimes thousands, of pictures before I complete my study of a person's feet. Clients return to the office day after day for more photos as I piece together clues about their condition. And I am just the photo technician. Step one. After the pictures they have to see the foot analyst, step two, and then my boss, the foot theoretician, step three. Even if he is vile in his life outside of work, the foot theoretician treats his clients well. I think. I don't really know. Not many clients have the patience to make it all the way to step three. Many of them claim to be better, if not cured, after a few sessions of photography.

It's not simple, and I take my time to do it right. It's possible that my boss admires my work. But that's not why he asked me to hug him yesterday. He is needy. He didn't say, "May I hug you?" He said, "Can I get a hug?" He solicited the appearance of a voluntary response, and then he reached his muscly arms all the way around me, and even though I stood there less sensate than the trunk of a tree, I hugged him. That's the nature of the power relationship. I used to have a girlfriend who would point to her cheek, tap twice with her index finger, and I would know that she wanted a kiss. When I kissed her she and I would both feel a thrill because she liked to control and I used to like to be controlled, at least by my lover. I don't like being controlled by other people anymore. Taking pictures of feet has changed me, or something else has.

Yesterday I was on my third round of photographs of the space between the big toe and the second toe, on the right foot of one of my clients. I've been seeing her for almost three years, and I have clear, useful material on most of her right foot, but until recently I was convinced that my work with her was only beginning. Her feet are complex and in pain. She was sixty-five when she first came for treatment, and in the months that I've been photographing her I've seen how the bones of her feet are drawing together, the ligaments are less flexible, and the skin on her feet is thinning while the feet themselves fluctuate in puffiness. Her condition might be caused by age, but I'm not an analyst or theoretician. I just take pictures as comprehensively as I can. Changes are undoubtedly occurring in other parts of her body as well, but I only work on feet.

This client is someone I think of as a foundational individual in society. Let's call her Etta. She has given birth to two children and raised them to adulthood while working full time at a job that supports a vital social institution. Compared to her, my boss, while powerful, is boring. Power without authority makes people tedious, and maybe even frightening. I think there was a philosopher who wrote about the banality of evil. Maybe it starts with the tedium of power. You probably didn't notice that I seemed to include you in the naming of this character, Etta, and in this paragraph I'm addressing you directly, giving you the feeling that you have some control over this story. You don't. But I don't want you to get bored. In this way a story, even a true story, is both the same as, and the opposite of, life. There should be a better word for this than paradox. You do have the choice to stop reading. I hope you don't.

The skin between the big and the second toe is usually easier to photograph than the skin between the other toes, because there's more skin there to start with, and most people are capable of spreading the big toe away from the other toes at a wider angle than they can spread the other toes away from each other. This is true for Etta, although sometimes the puffiness of her feet is an issue during photography; I ask her to grab her toes and stretch them away from each other using her hands. This isn't easy for her, even though she's sitting in a chair. She has a hard time bending far enough to reach her feet, and she becomes short of breath. When we reach to grab our toes we crunch up our lungs, and it is harder to breathe, unless you're a yogi and you can bend forward with a perfectly flat back.

Tamara Jaffe

Every part of the body is connected to every other part. I understand my client's body, so I wait for her to do what she usually does
when I ask her to hold her toes apart, which is to take a deep breath,
lunge toward her toes, and hold them apart while I take as many
pictures as I can, as fast as I can, until she lets go. She sits in the chair
while we perform this ritual, but it's difficult for her. If one day she
can no longer reach her feet, and I still need more pictures of the
interdigital skin, I'll place her toes in the adjustable toe separation
form. Most clients, including Etta, prefer to separate their toes by
hand. Before taking pictures I show each client the choices available
with my equipment; I match my technique to their needs.

A few months ago I began to understand that the skin between
Etta's big toe and her second toe was very important to her condition, and I might have seen this sooner if we'd spent a few more
days completing the pre-intake interview, but at the time it seemed
as if she had said everything she could say. There's no way to know.

Before I begin the work of photography I am part of the three-
person pre-intake interview committee. When you go for foot
analysis there are always three representatives on the pre-intake
interview committee because the three stages of the treatment
process—photography, analysis, and meta-analysis (theory)—require
different forms of information. I had a feeling that we were missing
some important questions at the time, but the foot analyst, and my
boss, the theoretician, both seemed satisfied that we knew what we
needed to know in order to begin. Now I see that wasn't true. That's
one of the characteristics of what is true. Most of the time we only
know it by what it isn't.

When Etta came to us for foot analysis she'd just retired from
working as a secretary in a school, and she still had good medical
insurance. In our pre-intake interviews we don't ask if a client
enjoys his or her work. Many of us enslave ourselves to obtain insurance, and everyone, including those in the foot analysis industry,
accepts this as inevitable. Insurance is the power to procure treatment, which could mean life or death, so it seems natural to go to
any lengths to obtain it. Even in retirement Etta had enough insurance to cover the first ten years of treatment. She figured that after

Andrea Begins to Speak

ten years her feet would be better, or not, but they couldn't be worse. I don't know if that's true. I've never had treatment.

I didn't begin to understand the significance of the changes in the skin between Etta's big toe and her second toe until after I'd begun the work of photographing her feet. Fortunately, Etta talks about her life while I'm working, and if I listen I can adjust my method to respond to the useful information she reveals. One day, near the beginning of her treatment, she spoke the following monologue, or something close to it:

> "I've always missed the students when they were on vacation, and then they graduate, and I never see them again, and it's like they're on vacation, but they never come back. I miss them real bad for a while, and I remember their names, and their voices, then they just slip out of my mind like they never existed."

Her voice slowed down, and decreased in volume quite a bit, so I wasn't sure if she wanted me to hear the next sentence or not. "Retirement is like that except it seems like I never existed."

When I heard this, I understood that her answer to one of our pre-intake questions, three years earlier, had been very incomplete. The analyst asked her a stock question, "What brought you in for treatment at this point in your life?" And she said, "I have the time and the insurance right now." We should have kept asking questions. The analyst and theoretician are sometimes satisfied with vague answers, probably due to the nature of their work, but I'm not. I did try. I said, "Well, it looks like you've had insurance for a long time. What changed?" Her answer was that work took most of her time and she'd never wanted to give up her free time for foot analysis. This was true, but so incomplete that it lacked most of the variables that contributed to her condition. Her retirement took her feet out of contact with the shoes and floors that had defined their previous existence, and we were remiss not to ask a single question about that.

Where people walk, sit, and stand for long periods of time, and what

Tamara Jaffe

materials are in contact with the surface of their feet, make all the difference when it comes to diagnosing their condition.

You might think that the only people who come for foot analysis are those with pain, or such distinct foot anomalies that it impedes buying shoes or walking. But most of our clients are humans with two feet, arches, and differentiated toes. There is a wide range of normal for this bipedal condition. Different people require treatment for different reasons. For Etta, it's pain, but that's not always the case.

In Etta's years of work at a school, her normal foot condition included a dress code, as well as hours of enforced sitting, both of which damaged the circulation in her feet. Having her as a client is one reason I returned to exercising.

The skin between Etta's great toe and her second toe has accommodated significant scarring since she began treatment. When she first came in she had to remove bandages from this spot. Bandages and socks impede photography. A client's feet must be bare during picture taking sessions. Etta had blisters between the big toe and second toe on each foot, and it was important to her to keep having blisters and cuts until she had toughened up this skin enough to wear sandals that had a toe separator there. A few weeks ago I asked her directly about the dress code at the school where she had worked, and her response confirmed my speculation. "No sandals" was part of the dress code.

It took me three years to understand that the scars between Etta's great and second toe are important to her condition, and directly linked to her fear of non-existence. Many of my clients are unaware of their fear of non-existence. Because foot therapy is very time intensive, they sometimes awaken to this fear in the middle of a session and become panicky. The program manager of foot psychophysiology keeps soothing drugs on hand for these moments. As a foot photography technician I am interchangeable with others like me, and if I stopped existing it would not be hard to find a replacement. I'm pretty sure this doesn't worry me. Perhaps we technicians strive for non-existence. The room where I work is very spare, and anyone could work there. It's on the first floor of the foot psychophysiology building at the University of Quincy, so I'm a university employee, although I don't get the same benefits as foot analysts, professors, or theoreticians. I'm in the employment category FTPT59741Q, the same as secretaries. We get free parking.

To facilitate clear photos there are no windows, mirrors, or reflective surfaces of any kind in my photography room. The walls and ceiling form a square cream-colored box with one domed light fixture in the center of the ceiling. Along the walls I have an assortment of lamps, footrests, and wooden shelves to store my gear. By the door there is an empty shelf and a wooden box for the client to store her or his things. In the center of the room there is a square white linen armchair with cushioned back and sides for clients to sit in while I photograph their feet. The floor of the room is smooth light oak, so that my clients and I can comfortably walk barefoot. I do not wear shoes when I work, to normalize my client's condition of being barefoot. In the foot photography technician training program instructors did not address the question of whether a photographer should be shod while working. I choose no shoes, and it is sometimes a comfort to my clients to view the syndactyly of my second and third toes. Like many people with syndactyly, my second and third toes are completely conjoined from the base to the distal interphalangeal joint, or top toe knuckle. While some euphemistically refer to syndactyly as webbing, it's a more serious and complete conjunction than that. Dan Aykroyd and Ashton Kutcher have syndactylic toes. So did Joseph Stalin. Etta admires my syndactylic toes.

Etta's intentional scarring between her first and second toes on each foot is not pathogenic, for a sixty-eight-year-old woman. Her need to wear sandals with a separator between the first and second toes likely places her condition in the category of aspiring mystic, as does the intentional scarring. I made this observation today, but medically it is almost entirely without weight. Until today I didn't know that my work with Etta is almost complete. If Etta continues treatment the analyst and theoretician will assist her, perhaps toward the goal of being pain free in her feet, but maybe not. Once a client understands her condition she is free to set her own goal in treatment. The analyst will explain to her how her symptoms reflect the four quarters of the universe, and if she continues to come for treatment the theoretician will open up to her the meaning of this condition. Etta already knows that her feet are complicated. She probably does not know that her condition is related to factors outside of her experience, connected to her precise location in space and time. Even the sandals that she chose to wear after having worked at a job forbidding such foot accoutrements have a history seemingly unrelated to Etta but intimately involved in her existence. I've never seen this exact condition before, but in foot photo technician training we studied it, and learned to recognize the signs. I spent many weeks photographing the interdigital skin between Etta's great toe and the next toe, first on the left foot, and then on the right, following the direction of my training. I blame myself for not identifying the intentionality of Etta's scarring earlier in the process. Many people scar their feet by wearing shoes that do not fit, but to do it on purpose matters.

In eastern traditions that predate religion, each quarter of the universe, earth, air, sky, and the realm beyond the sky, is one pada, or footprint. These padas seem unrelated to human existence but they represent an idea that something or someone touches this universe, creating boundaries. Intentional scarring, self-inflicted or prescribed by a community, reflects the human authority to manipulate a boundary. Once freed from the work regulations that controlled and defined her daily foot environment, Etta opened herself to communication with the context of existence by creating the cuts and blisters that became scars between her great and second toes. Her favorite sandals now fit her comfortably.

Through our feet we manifest our actions; the traditional paduka-style sandal that became important to Etta connects her to the oldest extant record of foot psychophysiology, contained in the Rigveda. I shouldn't have been surprised. The pada, foot, forms the foundational energy of our universe, and paduka footwear, a simple sole with a knob between the great and second toe, or a loop around the first toe, such as Etta favors, is one of the most ancient symbols of the relationship of the divine to the human.

Andree Begins to Speak

The self-inflicted scarification between Etta's great and second toes shows a deep commitment to freedom similar to that of early mendicants such as the Buddha. As a foot psychophysiology photo technician I am not trained to describe Etta's condition or its meaning to her, but I have studied the photographs and shared them with the foot analyst. If Etta chooses to continue her treatment she will soon begin sessions with the foot analyst.

Today will likely be my last photography session with Etta, and I will recommend that she advance to analysis. If she makes it to the final step, foot theory, I hope that my lonely boss will give her an accurate description of the meaning of her condition. Or maybe he'll quit before Etta completes foot analysis, and take a fancier job at a higher level. There's a fairly rapid turnover in the position of foot theoretician. He's the twelfth boss I've had.

After I leave work tonight I will stop by the gym to run and lift weights. I want my blood to circulate as best it can for as long as it can. The man I live with may or may not be in crisis; I can't take responsibility for that anymore.

II. Heaven

At the gym I use a long rubber band to attach a history of the royal courts of India to the eye-level shelf of my elliptical machine, to learn more about my work while I exercise. I'll get my heart rate up to 145 and try to keep it there for an hour, while I read. Sometimes I read fiction, but history is just as good, if it has good sentences. Foot psychophysiology began in India, and no matter how much we Westerners study we'll never reach the degree of accuracy that a simple village foot psychophysiologist in the Himalayas might have.

When I arrive home I see that the man I live with is reading, in his reading chair. He doesn't look up. Because it's 7 p.m. instead of 5:30 he knows I've been exercising. I know almost nothing about him. We started dating while I was in the foot photography technician training program, and moved in together shortly after I began my current job. I had no idea I'd enjoy my work so much that I'd keep this job for decades.

Tamara Jaffe

At home I don't change the cat litter or take out the garbage. The man I live with does that, and I do the cooking. Our house smells like coffee and soup. Tonight I'll bake more fish, with butter and garlic. Even though the man I live with was mad when I told him that I was exercising again he probably won't bring it up tonight. The radio is on a jazz station, as usual. Usually when I'm home, I turn it off. When the man I live with is home he turns it on. I'll leave it on. I have other things to think about.

I'll miss Etta. I have two other clients right now, but Etta has come in five days a week for the last few years. She might like analysis, I don't know, I don't get to talk to clients after they move to the next stage of treatment, and I don't know if she'll get to theory or not. This is the first time I've recommended that a client progress. Usually they drop out of treatment before I'm finished with my work. Our training program prepares us for that. It's normal.

I guess I don't know much outside of my work. The man I live with knows many things, like all the answers on *Jeopardy*, and he could probably work at several different jobs. I'm not clear about exactly what he does, but his job title is oral surgeon, and he makes about ten times what I make. I think he pulls teeth. I don't know if I could do that or not. I've never tried.

At night when we sit and read I still read fiction and history, and he reads books from all over the world. He likes books that have trains in them. He's read every African novel that has a train in it, and most of the British novels with trains. Lots of British detective works are set in or around trains. I read a few of the books he reads. But I still have a lot to learn just about the history of Asia, and I'm hardly ever in the mood for a mystery.

Did you know that when the Buddha stood up from under the bodhi tree his footprints remained imprinted on a stool, or on the earth? It depends on which story you read. Buddha's footprints are revered in many places. The four footprints of the creators define the earth, air, sky, and the realm beyond the sky. The padas. The feet leave behind a pattern that serves as the outline of the actions of the maker, and forms the basis for many beliefs. Not mine. I enjoy these stories, but when I photograph feet I attempt to communicate exactly what is in front of me, not an abstract idea. In Etta's case, the connection is clear. Her feet. Her freedom.

III. Hell

You might be wondering about the subtitles. When Vishnu walks, in three strides he covers the universe. In the first step he covers earth, in the second step he crosses heaven. In the third step he crosses hell. Some people worship Vishnu-pada, Vishnu's feet. I don't. And I could be wrong about Etta.

Tamara Jaffe

Life Underground

AVRA MARGARITI

I've recently joined this Facebook group where people around the world roleplay as ants—no, not like that. Nothing weird, just unusual. I suspect I enjoy feeling like I'm part of something.

I tried telling my therapist about the colony, but I could tell from the switching railroad tracks of her eyebrows that she didn't understand. So I talked about how I feel like I'm in danger even when I'm safe. How, in romantic relationships, I feel loved even when I'm not. Especially then.

I power up my home computer first thing after work. Sloane'82 posts: *A western tunnel has collapsed, anyant willing to help?*

Dig, go people in the comments. *Dig dig dig.* I type the three letters into the bar and hit send thinking, I did it. I accomplished something.

When I'm not in therapy, I make lists of things I should bring up next session. I saw my ex walking his dog and felt like gnashing my teeth at him but instead I made small talk and exchanged pleasantries. There was a fake bomb threat at the mall where I get almond-milk lattes even though I don't like the way they make my gums taste. At night I dream about sleeping in nests with the other ants, safe in the crowd, underground.

I should probably delete this last one.

An Australian named Robbie Fighter posts a picture of a red lollipop his toddler dropped on their lawn. *Anyant wanna help carry it to the colony?*

Lift, go the group members in the comments. *Lift lift lift.*

I stay up all night, burnt coffee and yellow streetlight, refreshing the page until dawn breaks and mends itself into morning. My voicemail blinks its angry red eye. My boss, or maybe an insurance salesman, like my ex. Or, why not, a bomb prank.

I pay it no mind, entranced by the sheer number of colony members responding. The lollipop must have made it safely underground by now. Everyant has been working so hard, they deserve a sweet treat.

My fingers tremble as they type. I know no-ant needs me, but it still feels good to be part of something.

Lift.

Ava Margaritt

No Man's Land

GRAHAM ROBERT SCOTT

When we round the corner, the boy in the purple shirt's already running.

Gunny punches the gas, cutting Hatch off mid-sentence. Orphaned syllables crackle over the speakerphone. Hatch can be a funny guy, but I think maybe he's funnier with his words chopped up and scattered to the airwaves. I can play Mad Libs in the caesura.

There are days, Gunny told me over burgers, back in my first week, when you'll be minding your own business and someone will react to your presence. To the car, to the uniform. They'll spin a U-turn, break into a run. Volunteer out of the blue to be pursued. When that happens, you thank the cop gods for the gift, and you don't lose them.

Indigenous scrub and cactus grid a patch of earth to our left the shade of sandpaper, the entirety palisaded by rows of trees. The area has a formal name, botanical commons or something, but for all its needles, guys on the force call it the Prick Yard, and that's where our jackrabbit goes, feet kicking up plumes of gravel from the garden path.

I call in the description. Lanky, long-legged, dark of skin. Purple shirt. Too young to buy cigarettes, old enough to try. The shirt had some kind of design on it, but he flew by too fast to catch it. My mind's eye instead conjures my father, smudged with grease, working with me on the Mustang, and I'm not sure why, but this ghost of the mind is a sock to the gut. I only snap out of it when Gunny yanks us into a sharp left into an alley that borders the eastern edge of the Yard, snarled epithets drowned out by the growl of tires over alley asphalt as pocked as the Moon.

Through the zoetrope blur of windbreak trees, the boy appears to flit across the park, cougar quick, while we loop the long way. As I open my mouth to predict we'll lose him, another blur catches my eye through the windbreak. A middle-aged woman, apparently after the boy on foot, mouth wide on a pink face, wide like she's shouting, and maybe she is. But what I hear as I watch her mouth, like *Bad Lip Reading*, is Hatch, still on speakerphone.

Whatever he's shouting sounds like a war cry.

Hatch lives for the chase. A regular at Gunny's barbecues, he entertains fellow LEOs with beer-thickened tales of Border Patrol night hunts, of illegals thumped into the sand with the wheel-well of a Jeep. My sister likes to say that in every community, the fastest way to accumulate social currency is to be mean to the right people. In ours, Hatch is aggressively upwardly mobile. Gunny looks the other way, most of the time. Sure, he's an asshole, Gunny reassured me one night before the drinking started, but he's our asshole. I stared at Gunny until he realized what he said, and then we both laughed for far too long.

Hatch yells that he's on the other side of the Yard and can see our rabbit heading his way.

I got 'em!, he shouts. I got 'em!

Hatch, I say. Stand down.

Maybe I'm not loud enough. Maybe Hatch doesn't hear me.

We corner, hard left out of the alley, back tires peeling around—

—as a white Silverado rams through the chain at the Prick Yard's service entrance and thumps the boy with its front left well.

Graham Robert Scott

The kid flies, arms windmilling, legs at weird angles, onto a nest of cotton-top cactus.

As we get out, Hatch is doubled over outside his truck, laughing, thrumming with adrenaline.

The boy doesn't move. He's face down, velcroed head to toe across a bed of pink spines. An earbud dangles outside his right ear. One purple sleeve tents to a sharp point, a dark wet shape welling into the cloth.

You can thank me later, Hatch calls to Gunny. Here comes the victim.

I see her, too, shrieking our way at a dead sprint. I can't make out the words, but her expression's all wrong. Her shirt's the same purple as the kid's, and now I can make out the design. Stenciled on its front, a human figure runs through a ribbon, head back and arms flown wide. Below the figure: the name of a high school from one town over.

Oh, I think, and then I throw up.

At home, I avoid news channels and social media. It's a local story at the moment, the union steward told me, but someone national is going to home in on it. The phone will start ringing, and people with microphones will ask why we didn't use a siren, why the kid kept running, why the kid hopped a hedge if he was just training, why, why, why. Don't answer, the steward said. Don't even pick up the phone. No answers you give will help anyone. No, not even the kid. But I keep returning to the image on the shirt, and to the last frame of a movie Dad watched days before his mobilization, eight months before his interment, about Australian track runners in the trenches of the World War I, one of whom dies sprinting across No Man's Land. The last frame finds him in the same pose as the runner on the shirt, but spouting bullet holes drilled by Turkish gunners. I spend hours trying to remember the name of the movie, until at last I have to look it up, and then I'm still awake, staring at the ceiling in the dark, mulling the word *Gallipoli* and how much it sounds like *gallop*, like gunfire, like tires over potholes, a perfect word that races by you and is then, in the smoke and the dust, forgotten.

No Man's Land

Down Along the Yocona

AUSTIN SHIREY

Me and Dewey Stokes sat reading in the shade on the porch of Flem's General Store drinking Coca-Cola and eating cheese and crackers. I was just about halfway through *The Once and Future King* when Vernon Parker rode up the street like the Devil was nipping at his heels.

"Anse!" he called, slick with sweat, knees pumping up and down like pistons. "Dewey!"

"Quit that hollering," I said.

Vernon hopped off his bicycle at the corner of the store and let it crash in the dirt next to our bikes. "Y'all never guess what I seen!"

"Flem shoo us off, you keep howling like that," Dewey said, closing his *Swamp Thing* comic and adjusting his glasses. His curly red hair looked like that bush that talked to Moses in the desert. "You know he only let us sit here long as we don't cause no ruckus."

"Awright, awright," Vernon said at a more acceptable volume, huffing like a bellows as he thundered up the steps to the porch. He was fourteen, just like me and Dewey, but he was bigger than both of us, built like a hibernating bear. "Can I get a drink?"

"Here," Dewey said.

Vernon downed the rest of Dewey's Coke, slumping his butt on the porch in between the rocking chairs we were sitting in. He leaned his shaggy brown head back against the wood siding of the store until his nose pointed skyward, then he closed his eyes and focused on catching his breath.

"Well?" Dewey asked.

"Well, what?"

I sighed and closed my book. "What the hell you hollering for?"

Vernon's eyes popped open. "I just said."

"You ain't said nothing."

"Didn't I?"

"Naw," Dewey said. "You ain't said nothing."

"Oh." Vernon's hazel eyes brightened. "There a gator down in the river."

"Ain't no gator in the Yocona," Dewey said. "You just seen a log or something."

"Naw. Was a gator, swear to God. Big ol' gator, too. Seen it from the bridge."

Dewey glanced over at me, blue eyes pleading for help. I shrugged and took a swig of soda. Beads of condensation flowed down the glass and through my fingers to splotch the gray wood between my black Converse high-tops.

"Got a knife stuck 'tween its eyes, too," Vernon said.

I arched an eyebrow, emptying my drink and chucking it into the trash can in the corner. *Clank.* "It what?"

"Gator got a knife in its face."

Dewey watched me, waiting.

I shrugged again. "Got nothing better to do."

It took us less than ten minutes to ride from Flem's down to the bridge. The July sun blazed in a bright blue sky, drenching us in sweat as soon as we'd left the coolness of the porch.

The bridge, where Lafayette County's main road crossed the Yocona River, was a neglected concrete line between a pair of hills covered in brown, sun-dead grass. The river itself was nothing but a winding scribble of muddy water.

We took a dirt path worn into the hill at the edge of the bridge and followed it down—right into someone pulling a johnboat out of the water.

"Whoa!"

I swerved right, nearly launching myself over my handlebars.

"God's sakes!"

Dewey veered left, barely missing Vernon.

"Watchit!"

Vernon slammed on his brakes, his bike bucking like a stallion as he skidded around Dewey and came to a stop at water's edge.

We sat coughing on the cloud of dirt our last-minute maneuvers had kicked up.

"Y'all okay?"

The hairs on the back of my neck danced.

That voice.

It was crystalline—like cool, clear water. Almost sing-song.

"Gwendoline Falk," Dewey whispered, like he was praying the name of Jesus.

She stood shimmering in glimmers of sunlight glinting off the river, dressed in a purple bikini top and muddied jean shorts. Golden hair dripped down freckled shoulders, framing a star-bright smile and gem-green eyes.

The day instantly felt hotter.

"Heya, boys," Gwendoline said, dropping her aluminum johnboat in the dirt. She placed both hands on her hips. "Haven't seen y'all since school let out."

"Uh, h-hiya," Dewey said, his voice catching in his throat. He pushed his glasses back up on the bridge of his nose.

Vernon looked everywhere but Gwendoline, his cheeks as red as apples.

I cleared my throat. "Hi, Gwendoline."

"Hi, Anse," she said, winking at me.

I felt my neck and face start burning with a heat that put the sun to shame.

Gwendoline Falk was fifteen, and as far as the three of us were concerned, she was the most beautiful girl in the whole wide world.

Austin Shirey

She was one-in-a-million, so unlike any of the other girls we knew, never afraid to tear or dirty her clothes hunting and fishing and hiking and boating. I always wondered if Gwendoline's wild nature had something to do with her mammy dying when she was little and her daddy raising her all on his own, or if it was just who she was. Maybe it was a bit of both.

"What y'all down here for?" Gwendoline asked. "Fishing ain't worth a damn today."

"Gator in the river," Vernon said.

"Knife 'tween its eyes," Dewey added.

"That so?" Gwendoline said.

We nodded.

"What y'all fixing to do with it? Catch it and pull the knife out?"

Me and Dewey and Vernon looked at each other with wild eyes. It was the greatest idea we'd ever heard.

"Yup," I said, surprising myself with the certainty I heard in my own voice. "That's the plan."

Dewey nodded. "Uh-huh. First one to pull the knife out, he, uh—"

"He be King of Lafayette County for the summer," I said, spitting out the first thing that came to mind.

Gwendoline laughed, and I wondered if stars sounded like that when they twinkled in the night. "Like King Arthur? Pulling Excalibur from stone?"

"Just like."

"Never figured you for much of a reader," she said, giving me another wink.

My neck and face burned red again and I looked down at my shoes. Of course she knew I liked reading—everyone did. Always had my nose in a book, like some kind of geek.

"How y'all fixing to catch a gator without no boat?"

My heart sank. I hadn't thought of that.

Dewey pulled off his glasses and wiped them clean with his shirt. They weren't dirty.

Vernon ran a hand through his hair.

"Hows bout I give y'all a ride in mine?" Gwendoline said.

I looked up at her. "Would you?"

Gwendoline beamed. "Sure! One condition, though."

"What's that?"

"Y'all let me in on your little game."

"Huh?" Dewey asked, pushing his glasses back on.

"I want in on your game," Gwendoline said. "I wanna be King of Lafayette County for the summer, if I can."

"But you're a girl," Vernon said.

I cringed.

"Oh, so a girl can't be king?"

"I reckon you'd make a great king," I said, immediately wishing I hadn't when her eyes sparkled back at me.

"Well, now," Gwendoline said. "Ain't you a sweetheart, Anselm Caruthers."

I gulped.

Gwendoline wafted toward me, smelling like freshly-squeezed lemonade.

It took everything in me not to ride away.

"Hows 'bout we make this more fun, huh?"

"H-how so?"

"Well, I figure a king need a queen, right? Say one of y'all strapping young men here pull that knife from the gator, be king for the summer. I'll be their queen. Their best girl. Give them their first kiss."

I couldn't breathe.

"But," Gwendoline said, holding up a finger. "I pull the knife out the gator, y'all be my menservants for summer. Y'all do my chores, do anything I want, anything I say. Treat me like a king." *123*

We all swallowed.

And one by one, we nodded.

Gwendoline clapped. "Good! Let's go get my knife!"

"Your knife?" I asked.

"You stuck the gator 'tween the eyes?" Vernon said.

"Yup! Was out this morning pulling up jug lines me and Paw set last night. Big black thing slide up to my boat when I's pulling

Austin Shirey

one in, ripped a big cat right off the hook, too. Did the only thing I could think of."

"Jab at its face," I said.

Gwendoline nodded. "Was my Mammy's knife, too. Thought I had to make peace with losing it, 'fore I ran into y'all."

She flashed me such a sad, puppy-dog look that I swore to myself right then and there that I'd do anything she ever asked of me.

"Holy hell," Dewey said, pointing toward the river.

Me and Vernon and Gwendoline followed his finger.

There, in the water, gliding like a long black log, tail swishing lazily back and forth, a black-handled fishing knife jutting out from between the two yellow eyes sliding along just above the water line, moved the biggest gator any of us had ever seen.

"Good God Almighty," I said.

"Bigger than I thought," Vernon said.

"Holy hell," Dewey said again.

Gwendoline jumped back to her johnboat and shoved it into the water. She turned, smiling like a cat that caught a mouse.

"Y'all coming or what?"

I was mesmerized watching Gwendoline navigate down the Yocona. She sat back at the engine, so cool and calm that I wondered if she'd been born on the water.

I imagined myself pulling the knife from the gator and holding it aloft like Excalibur; imagined Gwendoline wrapped around me and covering me with kisses, the sun setting orange and pink on the horizon; Dewey and Vernon kneeling in adoration.

It was glorious.

And then Gwendoline caught me staring like a fool, and I shot my eyes forward like they were bottle rockets, hoping I'd not let my gaze linger too long and wondering if I'd only imagined that hint of a smile at the corners of her mouth.

The gator flowed downriver letting the current do most of the work, seemingly oblivious to us trailing along in our sputtering little skiff.

"It's heading to the swamp," Dewey said over the buzz of the engine, his fiery hair licked and whipped by the wind of our passage.

Gwendoline nodded.

Dewey and Vernon shared a look. I knew what they were thinking: I'd been thinking it myself.

Swamp is gator country.

I'd much rather take the beast out on the open river, but judging from the set of her sinuous jaw, Gwendoline had no intention of stopping and waiting for it to come back upstream.

So I pretended I wasn't scared.

If riding out on the open river felt like being cooked in an oven, then riding through the swamp felt like being boiled. Even the shade did nothing to lessen the wet heat blanketing the swamp like a heavy, suffocating cloud that smelled of moldy foliage and bad eggs.

Gwendoline eased off the engine and grabbed the single oar lying lengthways in the boat, then paddled along in the gator's wake. The buzzing of insects grew loud in the absence of the engine's hum, and a chorus of croaking frogs and warbling birds surrounded us.

The swamp looked like a muddied mess of greens and browns; a living graveyard of trees and vines, logs and Spanish moss. Monster-sized skeeters soared through the air, dive-bombing our sweaty skin. Clouds of midges swarmed our faces, needling into eyes and barreling up noses. The water turned dark and thick in places, almost like molasses; water-bugs danced and swirled around floating leaves as they dodged the snapping mouths of hungry fish.

Gwendoline followed the gator around a bend where the river shallowed on our right, beneath the shadow of an ancient magnolia tree.

Here, the gator turned itself around and went still.

Gwendoline thrust the oar to the bottom of the river, slowing the boat to a stop a few feet from the monster.

Its yellow eyes glared up at us, as if to say:

Come and get me.

"So," Gwendoline said, "who goes first?"

I looked at my friends and swallowed. My mouth felt full of cotton.

Dewey cleared his throat and fiddled with his glasses. "Uh, shouldn't we, uh, figure how we gonna do this before, you know...we do it?"

"What's to figure out? Everybody take a turn grabbing at the knife. First one to pull it out, wins."

"Naw," I said, scratching at a skeeter bite on my arm. "Dewey's right. Can't just jump in. We need a strategy, or something."

"Okay. So what's our strategy?"

"Well," Dewey said, "first I reckon we, uh, best pull the boat up to the bank there, maybe attack from land?"

I nodded. "That's good thinking. Don't want to be in water with a gator, no how."

Gwendoline huffed as the boat rocked back and forth. "Y'all taking the fun out, sitting—"

"Excalibur!" Vernon bellowed, launching himself off the boat and over the gator, raising a log above his head like a bludgeon. Where the hell had he picked that up? And when?

"What in the hell?" Gwendoline said.

Vernon brought the log down on the gator with a heavy *whump* seconds before landing on top of it with a magnificent splash. Brackish water erupted like a geyser, showering all of us.

The water frothed white like a waterfall, and me and Dewey screamed and swore ourselves purple, eyes wide and gleaming, veins straining in our throats and foreheads.

Vernon's arm shot out of the water swinging the bog-log up and down in wild, violent arcs. The gator's black-scaled tail writhed up and out like a sea-serpent, cracking down over Vernon's skull and disappearing underwater.

The battle grew strangely distant, and I turned to find Gwendoline guiding the boat backward into the opposite riverbank with quick, panicked strokes.

"What the hell you doing? Vernon need us!"

"I know! But we gotta do it from solid ground, like you's said!"

"Hell, naw!" Dewey roared, and then he threw himself over the bow.

"Dewey!" I shouted.

I turned to look at Gwendoline again, felt the boat run aground.

And then I jumped overboard.

Everything was warm and murky and my heart thrummed like an engine in my chest as I surfaced.

"Anse!"

Gwendoline was screaming, but I hardly heard her over the roar of Vernon and Dewey and the gator.

I tried standing on the river bottom, but the swamp muck gave beneath me and I was sucked back under.

My lungs burned.

I panicked. I flailed my arms and legs, willing myself in the direction I hoped was up. I couldn't be sure, though: my bearings were completely bungled.

When I breached the surface, I sucked in a lungful of air, then doggie-paddled to the wild splashes directly ahead of me.

Someone's leg hit the side of my face, dunking me again. Arms and legs collided with me from a thousand different directions.

Something large and scaly *thumped* against my back. Claws or teeth sliced along my arm, scratched across my chest. The wounds stung, instantly reminding me of that one summer I'd been all pricked apart by hornets after Vernon had bombarded their hive with rocks.

All I heard was the pounding, percussive booms of my heart and the frantic splashes of my friends as they surely died, shred apart by razor-sharp teeth.

Something smooth passed through my hands and I grabbed it and then I was above water. I sucked in air, choking on a mouthful of river.

Gwendoline's screams floated like half-remembered ghosts

along the edges of my consciousness, but I had no time to figure out what she was saying.

I pushed forward, wrapped my arms around something human and then tugged it backward in the direction of the johnboat.

Something snapped at my shoes, but I kicked hard and kept swimming.

I swore I felt the gator's breath on my heels as I made my way back to Gwendoline as fast I could.

I pushed the body out of the river and into the boat, knocking Gwendoline onto her back; then I climbed in and stumbled over both of them.

There was a splash behind us and the boat heaved and suddenly Dewey was there, too.

The boat rocked back and forth as we pulled this way and that in a cussing mad effort to separate into whole, individual beings.

"My glasses!" Dewey cried as I pulled Gwendoline up from under Vernon. "Can't barely see a damn thing!"

"Vernon?" Gwendoline asked.

He wasn't moving.

"No, no, no," I said, flipping Vernon over. I smacked his cheeks, then hit his chest when that didn't wake him. "C'mon, Vernon! Wake up! Wake up!"

"Move," Gwendoline said, pushing me aside.

She straddled Vernon, pinching his nose, placing her mouth over his. She breathed, then pumped his chest with her hands.

Pinch, mouth, breathe, pump.

Pinch, mouth, breathe, pump.

Pinch, mouth, breathe, pump.

Pinch, mouth—

Vernon startled back to life, vomiting up swamp water and knocking Gwendoline back onto Dewey.

"Vernon!" I cried, and then me and Dewey tackled him to the bottom of the boat.

"Get offa me!" Vernon said. "Hurt like hell enough without y'all help, dammit!"

Down Along the Yocona

"Oh my God," Gwendoline said, falling onto a bench, wrapping her arms around her knees and hugging them to herself. "Oh my God."

Me and Dewey helped Vernon to his feet. Our arms and legs were covered in a dozen red scratches, but Vernon's clothes were absolutely shredded.

"You okay?" Dewey asked, squinting at Vernon.

"Reckon so," Vernon said, checking himself. "Ain't cut deep."

"Good," Dewey said, then socked him hard in the shoulder. "What the hell you thinking, jackass?"

"Ow! God, Dewey, I was just thinking what we all was thinking!" He looked sheepishly at Gwendoline and turned redder than a tomato.

Gwendoline looked away, and I thought I might've seen tears trickling down the curves of her cheeks.

"Anybody get the knife?" Dewey asked.

Vernon picked wet moss and dead leaves from his hair. "Naw. Think I had it for a moment, maybe. Musta dropped it. Sorry, Gwendoline."

"Oh," Gwendoline said, avoiding Vernon's eyes. "Th-that's okay, Vernon. Honest. Just glad you okay."

As I fingered the hilt of the knife where I'd slipped it under my shirt in the band of my shorts before coming back aboard, Gwendoline's screams coalesced in a surge of clarity:

"It's not my mammy's knife! It's not even mine! I was just playing with y'all! I didn't think y'all go this far, not for some stupid kiss!"

I hesitated; glanced at Gwendoline and then Dewey and Vernon.

And decided I'd had enough adventure for one day.

129

Austin Shirey

Nothing Plays Itself

JUAN CARLOS REYES

I set the pump in place. I told my kids to listen to their mother. I returned the debit card to my wallet and then crossed the divider, and then I almost returned to the van for my sweater. My double-take, first turning back to the van and then turning back toward the convenience store once I figured it wasn't that cold, I ended up spinning in the middle of the gas station, and two guys leaving the store shouted that if I liked dancing so much I should probably do it in a disco.

I watched them walk away as I walked to the front door they'd left open. I didn't smile and they didn't smile back, and neither of us pump faked the other like anybody was edging for a fight. I was just confused. I don't know anyone who calls anything a disco anymore.

The hesitation outside had me holding the door for a woman leaving the store, sipping on her soft drink as she tried to thank me past the straw. And then a squeal shook my skin alive, something of a jerk into and out of my arms, and I let the door go.

An old man had started playing the harmonica as he leaned against the beam that upheld the overhang. I grew up on street music, and my body, squared shoulders and all, has always faced the music, even when it encounters the pavement faster than the shock of it can skip off a bumper and skirt my legs.

Growing up, in the subway, on the bus, on platforms boiled by the summer and emboldened by the winter, and on street corners that found ways to go unnoticed even when lights flashing behind a violinist or cellist competed with the notes, my body always tensed with the strain of a contrast.

But nowadays I feel like a voyeur. I don't always pay a musician anymore. I don't carry change on me anymore, and the man's hands, shivering as he blew through the reed plates, as he held onto the cover plates like his fingerprints could leave impressions in the metal, felt like they needed gloves. His pants looked like they needed a wash. His boots held no laces, and he used a rope for a belt, and there I went again. I was sizing him up. He left no cup at his feet, and the breeze didn't necessitate a hat. But I sized him up anyway.

Shame is an interesting thing. You don't always know why you have it, and I didn't know if an ice cream had been enough to hand him after I left the store, but I figured to offer him what *I* would want. All that prefaced, of course, by the presumption that he'd wanted anything at all, and then that a hotdog and vanilla-chocolate bar would do, that it wouldn't have reminded him of something better or even worse.

But I figured I couldn't go wrong by giving something hot and also something cold.

When I got into the driver's seat, my wife asked me what I'd been measuring. She said my eyes get a certain way when I process the distances between people, whether or not I draw any certifiable lines between them.

I shook my head and said it was nothing. I said I was just covering all my bases. I got the kids each a different thing, and I got her and I each a different thing. I figured, however we mixed our matches, our hands would dance their way to some kind of agreement.

They'd find their way.

The Headless Army of Charlie Close

DIE BOOTH

They come in three sizes—small, medium and large—beheaded bodies, lining up in daily ranks on the waxed-shiny workbench. A headless army. Charlie imagines them like that: ready to stand up in defence at the next wrong word, their small solid ghost forms, like precursors to a truth, blockading the marauders outside.

There's a quality system too, that you must adhere to. The kid leather hides come ready-cut, a jigsaw of pieces that need to be matched according to the minutest gradations of shade and grain. The smoothest down *this* end, the coarser down *that*. Charlie is quick. Can sew up a pattern in minutes, the tiniest stitches binding seams neat as the lines on your palm, but the quality system seems meaningless: every body, they all look the same; all headless, sexless. Featureless ranks of them without variation.

"Miss Close."

There is a *no* in there somewhere, but it's hard to voice, too slippery and stabbing to pin down. Charlie says, "Ma'am?"

"You're a good worker, Lottie, but you need to pay more attention." Charlie's eyes follow as Mrs Smith moves a body, pointedly, from the top end of the row to the bottom. Flaccid limbs flop, off at the elbows. A casualty of war. Mrs Smith says, "There are any number of girls your age would be very thankful of three shillings a week. Do not count yourself irreplaceable."

"Lottie!" When Mrs Smith's back is turned, Sarah leans in and whispers, "That's twice this week!" Her pale curls bob, silky as cobweb.

Charlie hisses, "*Charlie.*" But if Sarah hears, she doesn't let on.

Charlie is not irreplaceable: this much is known. The cobbles are slick and tricky beneath boot soles as Charlie tramps home in a fine mist of rain, the type that hangs in the air almost unseen, unnoticed 'til it's soaked you through already. Charlie is as replaceable as any of the anonymous bodies on the workbench; Mother makes that clear as misty drizzle. Behave and be grateful, she says. Be thankful you're a part of something, a well-oiled cog in a smoothly-running machine, serving a useful purpose. We all have our part to play.

Parts. That's the problem. Charlie never gets to see the whole. Sometimes you get to sew composition arms in at the elbows— avoiding the finicky stitching of fingers—to stuff the bodies tight with straw. But they still all look the same: unclothed, identical, unidentifiable. Charlie never gets to see the heads. Never gets to see them fully assembled, never knows what they'll become. Once, there was an arm with a broken finger and the whole doll was tossed into the rubbish. Faceless and worthless. Charlie worries a thumbnail between grinding teeth and lifts the latch of the back door.

Inside, the fire is dying. Heels clicking across the kitchen flags, Charlie gives the embers a stir with the iron, coaxes them back into quietly crinkling elegy. It does little for the chill in the room, but it makes the light jump a shade more warmly. A check of the teapot, the kettle settled on its hook in the hearth, until Charlie can wrestle the cloth-wrapped handle to pour scalding water on the mulch of leaves that have been brewed it's-anyone's-guess-how-many times already today. It's not fair that the first one up, the last one home, the longest hours worked, gets the last cup, but that's how it is. And the tea's still good, however weak.

Charlie wraps cold hands around the teacup and breathes in

steam. The rain outside makes no discernible sound, but the fire sounds like rain, pattering. The little ones are already in bed. Mother too, maybe, or perhaps she's in the sitting room but Charlie doesn't care to check: better to be as quiet as the whispering flames, and creep up the stairs unseen to sleep. If Ann or Tilly wake at the noise, Mother won't come to question, not this late. Three to such a tiny bedroom is uncomfortable, but Charlie was moved out of the smallest room when John turned thirteen. It was no longer *seemly* to share. How it's any worse than with the girls, Charlie doesn't quite know, but keeps quiet and fights nightly for a share of quilt. There are more enticing prospects than a cramped cot, despite the weight of sleep pressing on Charlie's eyelids. Hot tea will cure all. The steam from the cup ghosts in lazy twists, sparks the vision of dancing figures, imagined in the shadowed street outside. All headless.

Charlie turns a hand, stares, as if the future can somehow be divined in the palm-lines that criss-cross like seams. There's a cross-hatch of slices, webbing old scars between first and second pointer-finger joints. Most are shallow, the merest scratch, but one is still weeping and red. Charlie presses the corresponding thumb against it: it stings. The needles you must use for leather are wicked little things, flattened to razors at the tips, designed for piercing flesh. Even so, Charlie can never work out where the cuts come from, exactly how the needle passes that causes it to break skin in that manner. None of the other doll-makers suffer it. It's encouraged to wear thimbles, or wrap scraps of leather around your fingers, but that slows you down, renders you clumsy. And Charlie suspects that it's more for fear of blood getting on the merchandise than any concern for the workforce. It's just easier to be careful, and if you can't be careful, be canny. Just once did Charlie slip up. The spot of blood, bright on white kid, is as stark a memory as the mistake was startling. Recalled, clear as if it was minutes ago, a vivid pinprick at the edge of one shoulder seam, not quite central enough to mark the point where a heart would beat. Looking down, Charlie had seen, in the uncertain gaslight, that same red recurring slice patterning that same finger. Perhaps there should be a pulse of panic: the memory brings none, and there was none at the time. Just the dull ache of sameness. A blunt throb like a heartbeat in the cut. Charlie remembers licking the tip of another finger, rubbing across the stain: erased well enough in the crease of the seam that the crime slipped past Mrs Smith's searching eyes. And somewhere out there is a doll with a little life in it, the invisible traces of blood and spit and breath. Charlie wonders, is it still the same as all the others? Or something, magically, different?

Charlie thinks of that doll from time to time. Wonders what it looks like, where it is. If it is beloved, or buried at the bottom of a tip heap, wearing Charlie's face.

There's a light burning in the sitting room, which calls for extra care. Past the entrance on tiptoe, and the stairs creak unhappily beneath wary feet. The door to Mother's room is shut, but the other two are cracked ajar, slipping small sounds of slumber. Charlie loiters on the unlit square of landing, shifting silently from one foot to the other. Reluctant to enter the obligation of that dreaming, sister-inhabited room. Are there two curly heads, resting there on the pillows? The urge to check is strong, but the light struggling in through the window is too weak to see by. Despite a long day at the workshop, sleep is suddenly distant. Very quietly, Charlie turns, and slips in through the opposite door instead.

This room is, even now, more familiar than the one shared with the girls. Every inch committed to memory, Charlie steps over each creaky floorboard and kneels before the chest at the foot of the bed. John is fast asleep. He's always slept like the dead. The quilt rises and falls, steady and almost imperceptible, with the quiet shush of his breath. The bed looks huge with only one occupant: lucky boy. Although he's two years Charlie's junior he's tall for his age and they're much the same size. When the lid of the chest inches open, the hinges are oiled enough to be silent: a blessing. Sorting through by touch alone, Charlie pulls out trousers, a shirt. Stands and slips quietly out of frock and petticoats and pulls on borrowed clothes over stockings and shoes.

The light is out in the sitting room when Charlie sneaks back down the stairs. John's cap hangs on a peg in the kitchen. Charlie puts it on, and leaves the back door on the latch.

Town past midnight is hushed in a way that makes Charlie long to whoop and run. The urge is containable, barely. Self-preservation is a must. Still—this feeling of triumph, of lightness: as if your feet could just lift off the pavement, float away.

It's still spitting that fine saturation of rain. It glitters in the gaslight like fog, magnifies the pricking lamps to coronas. Every noise out here is magnified too, hollowed into echo, a set of invisible feet mimicking footsteps next to Charlie's, keeping company all the way to the shop.

Not the workshop. The shop. It lies at the other end of the street from the rooms where the dolls are made, a jewel-box frontage shiny with new paint, only for the valuable children with the wealthy papas. Gawkers, from experience, are soon shooed away. Charlie has never seen the place at night before. In the dark, certainly—those early winter dusks where the sun is defeated at four and darkness has wiped the fire from the sky before it's time for home—but never like this. Not truly at night, when there might be no other people left in the whole world, when everything trembles on the edge of real.

Being clever with your hands has multiple advantages. A needle, an awl—carefully, Charlie slots the slim point of metal into the keyhole, wriggles it with a noise like clinking glass. Something gives. You need smaller hands than most to fit through a letterbox. The hard angle of metal catches against the crook of Charlie's elbow, the stiff bristles of the slot snagging against shirtsleeve. Another prod with the awl and the key drops free into Charlie's waiting palm. This is something serious. Something the police would take an interest in, out here in the open, not even at the backdoor of the building. But in this night-lit in-between, consequences feel imaginary. As if even were a policeman to come striding along the street, he wouldn't see what was before his own eyes.

It's not like Charlie's going to actually steal anything, after all. The bell tinkles on its spring as the door is eased open, cradled carefully to. Inside the shop is silent, like the building has inhaled in shock. The walls feel close. Warm. Charlie paces the floor, eyes the toys in their glass-fronted cases, on their neat shelves, sheltered in shadow. What little light makes it through the bow window is insufficient; in here, it's truly almost dark. Charlie inches further, towards the back of the shop, into the mute gloom. Where are the dolls? But of course—there they are. An entire counter of them, stretching the length of the rear of the room. A little army—no longer headless, featureless, anonymous—they parade in ranks, small, medium, and large, decked in ribbons and ruffles and lacquered leather shoes. Charlie shuffles to a halt, considering them. Each one is different now, dressed individually, a contrasting shade of silk for her frock, a complementary spray of flowers in her hair above a mild, uninterested stare. Each one is exactly the same: sweet-faced and friendly, with Sarah's blue eyes, her yellow curls. A legion of little girls who all started out blank, the same. A legion that Charlie helped to create. There are so many of them their faces seem to blur, to swim in the dim light. Something—a movement—catches the eye. For a moment Charlie thinks it's imagination, but there it is again; motion. The blink and startle of a pale face, reflected in the glass door of a cabinet. Charlie's face. Charlie takes a step towards it. Mirrored in the black glass, a backdrop of miniature girls look back. Charlie, amongst them, in trousers and shirt and hat. They are not all the same, after all. One of these things is not like the rest. Charlie nods and doffs his reflected cap. He closes the door quietly, turns the key in the lock and posts it back through the letterbox. He steps into the night.

138

Contributors

Niamh Bagnell lives in East Cork, and has been previously published in the Stinging Fly magazine, the Honest Ulsterman and Southword. She has twice read at Cork's International Short Story Festival. She is almost the only Niamh Bagnell in the world, so is easily found online. Upcoming stories appearing in *Antithesis* from Melbourne University, *Wilderness House Literary Review*, and *The Waxed Lemon*.

Aiden Baker lives in South Florida, where she teaches, writes, and gets really sweaty. You can find her work in *Ninth Letter* and *The Sonora Review*.

Die Booth is from Chester, UK, and likes exploring dark places and telling lies. You can read his stories in places like *Lamplight Magazine*, *The Fiction Desk* and *Fireworks*. His books *My Glass is Runn*, *365 Lies* (profits go to the MNDA) and *Spirit Houses* are available online, and a new collection of weird tales *Making Friends (and other fictions)* will be out soon. http://diebooth.wordpress.com/ @diebooth.

Swathi Desai is a creative director in the design industry and a graduate of the Wharton School. Her work has been published in *Prometheus Dreaming*, the *San Francisco Examiner Magazine* and elsewhere. She lives in the Bay Area with her family.

Stephanie Dickinson lives in New York City with the poet Rob Cook and their senior feline, Vallejo. Her novels *Half Girl* and *Lust Series* are published by Spuyten Duyvil, as is her feminist noir *Love Highway*. Other books include *Heat: An Interview with Jean Seberg* (New Michigan Press), *Flashlight Girls Run* (New Meridian Arts Press), *The Emily Fables* (ELJ), *Girl Behind the Door* (Rain Mountain Press), and her just-released *Big-Headed Anna Imagines Herself* (Alien Buddha). Her stories have been reprinted in *New Stories from the South*, *New Stories from the Midwest*, and *Best American Nonrequired Reading*. At present she's finishing a collection of essays entitled *Maximum Compound* based on her longtime correspondence with inmates at the Edna Mahan Correctional Facility for Women in Clinton, New Jersey.

Wynne Hungerford's work has appeared in *Epoch*, *Blackbird*, *The Brooklyn Review*, *American Literary Review*, and *SmokeLong Quarterly*, among other places. She received her MFA from the University of Florida.

Tamara Jaffe loves to think, read, write, and sometimes speak. For love and livelihood she teaches, no matter where she lives, or with whom, or how many children she has. She has published a few articles and chapters about teaching, and a bit of satire, under a couple of different names. This is her real name, but Audree and psychophysiology are invented.

Naomi Bess Leimsider has published poems and short stories in *Hamilton Stone Review, Rogue Agent Journal, Coffin Bell Journal, Hole in the Head Review, Newtown Literary, Otis Nebula, Quarterly West, The Adirondack Review, Summerset Review, Blood Lotus Journal, Pindeldyboz, 13 Warriors, Slow Trains, Zone 3, Drunkenboat,* and *The Brooklyn Review.* She teaches creative writing at Hunter College.

David Luntz's poems, short stories, and flash fiction have appeared in *Euphony, Word Riot, Andromeda Spaceways, Punchnels, The Journal of Compresed Creative Arts,* and other print and online publications.

Avra Margariti is a Social Work undergrad from Greece. She enjoys storytelling in all its forms and writes about diverse identities and experiences. Her work has appeared or is forthcoming in *SmokeLong Quarterly, The Forge Literary, Longleaf Review, The Journal of Compressed Creative Arts,* and other venues. Avra won the 2019 Bacopa Literary Review prize for fiction. You can find her on twitter @avramargariti.

Natasha Markov-Riss just graduated from Swarthmore College (via YouTube Livestream), where she studied Film and Media, Peace and Conflict, and Political Science. She is a big *30 Rock* fan, and her favorite authors include Virginia Woolf, Elena Ferrante, Ivan Turgenev, and Toni Morrison. Natasha will embark on a Fulbright to the Canary Islands next year, where she hopes to learn the whistling language!

Kevin McLellan is the author of *Hemispheres*, *Ornitheology* (which received honors at the 19th Annual Massachusetts Book Awards), [*box*], *Tributary*, and *Round Trip*. He won the 2015 Third Coast Poetry Prize and Gival Press's 2016 Oscar Wilde Award, and his writing appears in numerous literary journals including *Colorado Review*, *Crazyhorse*, *Kenyon Review*, *West Branch*, *Western Humanities Review*, and *Witness*. Kevin lives in Cambridge, Massachusetts. https://kevmclellan.com/

James Morena earned his MFA in Fiction at Mountain View Grand in Southern New Hampshire. His stories have been published in *Amoskeag Journal, Forge Journal, Rio Grande Review* and others. He also has published essays and poems. James teaches English at university and high school levels. You can interact with him on Insta: @james_morena.

Juan Carlos Reyes has published the novella *A Summer's Lynching* (Quarterly West) and the fiction chapbook *Elements of a Bystander* (Arcadia Press). His fictions and essays have appeared in *Florida Review*, *Waccamaw Journal*, and *Moss Literary Journal*, among others. He is the chief editor of *Big Fiction Magazine*, and he teaches creative writing at Seattle University. You can find him online at www.jcreyes.net.

143

Graham Robert Scott grew up in California, resides in Texas, and owns neither surfboard nor cowboy hat. By day, he's an English professor and assessment specialist at Texas Woman's University. His short fiction has appeared in *Pulp Literature, Barrelhouse Online, Nature*, and others.

Melissa Sharpe lives outside of Detroit and works in higher education. Being a parent to two has replaced most of the things that were interesting about her. Melissa has previously been published in *Redivider, Pennsylvania English, Zygote in my Coffee*, and *3288 Review* among others. You can follow her on Instagram @melissasawthis or melissa-sharpe.com.

Austin Shirey has been telling stories ever since he first read *The Hobbit* as a kid. If he's not writing, he's probably reading or enjoying time with his wife and daughter in Northern Virginia. His fiction has appeared in *All Worlds Wayfarer Literary Magazine, Stonecoast Review, Blind Corner Literary Magazine*, and is forthcoming in Eerie River Publishing's dark fantasy anthology, *With Blood and Ash*. Follow him on Twitter @tashirey87 and online at www.austinshirey.com.

Honor Vincent's poetry and stories are published or forthcoming in *Yes Poetry, Heavy Feather Review, Strange Horizons, Entropy, Neologism*, and elsewhere. She's currently writing a comic series about Boudicca and her daughters. She's a third generation New Yorker who lives in Brooklyn. You can find her work at https://www.rhonorv.com/words.

The Orcans

Publisher/Editor Joe Ponepinto's latest novel, *Mr. Neutron,* was published by 7.13 Books in 2018. He was the founding publisher and fiction editor of *Tahoma Literary Review.* He has had stories published in dozens of other literary journals in the U.S. and abroad, and has won a couple of contests.

Publisher/Editor Zachary Kellian is an author of flash fiction, short stories, and novels. He has been published in various journals and was a finalist for the Ernest Hemingway Foundation's Short Story of the Year in 2016. His non-fiction writing career has included work as a contributor for *The Huffington Post* and *Buzzfeed.* He recently concluded a national public-speaking tour on the complexities of intergenerational communication.

Co-Editor Renee Jackson is a multi-disciplinary artist currently splitting time between the US and Argentina. She has a passion for new work and a background in theatre where she has had the pleasure of assisting in the literary development and staging of several plays including (Non)Fiction (Jillian Leff), The Wildling (CJ Chapman), Minotaur (Teagan Walsh-Davis), and Gothic Arch (Jeffrey Fiske).

Readers

David Anderson is a writer of short fiction. While primarily focusing on short stories, his interest in flash fiction sparked while studying at Hugo House in Seattle. A recent finalist in a national flash fiction competition, he continues to study and challenge himself within a small group of emerging writers. David has also been a panelist at Pacific Northwest Writers Conference and Emerald City Comic Con.

Thomas Kenneth Anderson was born in South Bend, Indiana, raised in Romeo, Michigan, and currently resides in Tacoma, Washington. He's a Western Michigan University graduate working as a paper engineer. His focus is on flash and short fiction, with a background in journalism and satire. He enjoys mountains, beaches and fantasy baseball.

Zoë Mikel-Stites is a freelance fiction author and copywriter. With a background in theater, she had the chance to study visual story-telling, and the interaction of story and audience up close. She has a passion for science fiction and fantasy, and any medium that can tell a good story.

Ronak Patel is an educational researcher, telling stories through data. His research interests include racism in education and the model minority myth, and he has published work for non-profits, school districts, and state agencies in Washington and Hawaii. He also writes fiction and is currently exploring the South Asian American experience.

Marci Pliskin writes fiction and non-fiction. Her work has appeared in *Cottonwood* (University of Kansas) and on MSNBC.com. She lives with her family in Seattle. She is a 2019 New Millennium Writers Finalist in Non-Fiction.

Isabel Armiento (staff emeritus) studies English at the University of Toronto, where she is Editor-in-Chief of a campus newspaper and actively involved in several other campus publications. Her work has been published or is pending publication in *Submittable, The Mighty Line, Adroit Journal, Antithesis Journal*, and elsewhere, and she was a winner of the Hart House Literary Competition for prose fiction.

A LITERARY JOURNAL

Orca is about fiction. Short stories and flash. We are a literary journal and we believe in the literary style of writing.

We still believe writing can be fun, too.

Orca is published three times a year. The March and November issues contain literary work, some of which includes speculative elements, and July is our designated literary-speculative issue.

All the work we publish comes through the submission portal.

Fiction published in *Orca* may be nominated for anthologies such as *Best American Short Stories, Best Small Fictions*, the Pushcart Prize, and others. In our first year one of our stories was selected for *Best Canadian Short Stories of 2020.*

149

We are open year-round for submissions.
For complete guidelines please visit our site at orcalit.com